"Arctic Island Mist"

© Rolly A. Chabot

November 1st, 2012

Book One of Three

"Dedication"

There are times in life when life itself takes those that we love. We can choose to be bitter, we can choose to mourn and yet deep inside we find life again.

I dedicate this to a man whom I have known since 1985.

Dennis Norman, a mentor, a dear friend and a man who knew the true value of family, the value of life and the meaning of friendship.

To you Dennis and to you his family I dedicate the efforts of this writing. Somewhere while reading this may you find peace. Todd Morris is the main character in this book. Some of his qualities and his personality I drew from Dennis. May each of you know the many moments of great joy that he brought to us all. Above all during your loss, please know that you are dearly loved.

By no means is this a story of Dennis's life. The only similarity being the heart Todd Morris had has so much reminded me of Dennis.

Know that Dennis lives through us all through what we learned from him in loving and caring for those left behind.

You will be dearly missed but Dennis know that your spirit lives through all who's lives you touched. Thank you for caring and the many great memories...

Rolly A. Chabot

http://www.amazon.com/Rolly-A.-Chabot/e/B005HFAYGI

Woodcarver2009@me.com

Prologue

Injustice can harm a man far greater than man can do harm to himself. The pains of the past can rob and steal a man of who he was determined to be in life.

Such was the case with Todd Morris. His life and circumstances had brought about far to many hurts to repair. He had run from his past in search of what his future held.

Come along and travel with Todd as he begins to rebuild and regain what he once had. At least that is the way the average man would think.

This is no average man Todd has a different story, a story filled with a blank. A period of time where he lost reality of who he truly was. Little did he know his life would be the way it turned out.

Chapter One

"Before"

Tundra is what they called it. Void of anything is what he thought the first time he set foot on it. Far different than the sands of the western California coast line he had grown up in. Sand that moved under foot. Tundra moved underfoot alright, only a black gooey mess. One step would find you on solid ground and the next sliding. The only thing holding it together was the moss, lichen and a few shrubs. He hated it at first but this is where life had taken him at least for the time being.

"Not even a bloody tree to take a leak against." He turned in disgust from the window of the place he had been given to call home. His coffee had already gone cold in small two room trailer he had been given as a home, the furnace ran day and night. The temperature today a bone chilling 48 below zero. "Stupid country, what are you doing here fool? He heard himself say as he turned from the bleak scene outside.

Todd Morris was 44, 6 foot 6 inches, 300 pounds of pure muscle and brute strength. He was rough and tumble and had come to be known in the north as "Nanuq." (Inuit for Polar Bear) He was good natured at the best of times but should you cross his path well you might as well be trying to eat a mother bears cub. It was then you learned quickly to not make that mistake again.

His thoughts were broken at the sound of the annoying clock he had bought at the local trading post. Every hour had a bird beside it. They were the Birds of Canada and each time it struck the hour it would belt out the racket the bird would make. It was "Owl Hour" in plain english that was 3 in the morning. He hated that fool clock.

Restless nights where he could not sleep had become a part of life. It had been happening far to often of late. The time and climate change had taken their toll. He never was one to take pills, let alone ones to help him sleep. Todd Morris had been down that road with booze and drugs, prescription and the illegal ones. Look where it had led him. His way of thinking was go long enough without sleep and you will eventually get sleep.

He sat back in his chair and looked around his new settings and sighed. "You had it all Morris, now look at you and where you are."

His mind drifted back to better days in a small town called Dorchester just outside of Dallas. He had owned a thriving flight business there and had many contracts with different oil companies. His corporate office was in Dallas but his personal life was lived outside of the city.

He had all a man could ask for, a beautiful wife, Marie. They had two children. Lynsey was his oldest at 14, his son Jeff was 12. His family was who he worked for. They had meant the world to him. His home was the envy of most of the people in the county with acres of manicured lawn and gardens. In the good times he was a gambler. In his business if you were willing to go big and put on the dog, you got the work. No room for small time operators.

He had gone big after a few years of just getting by. He took a chance and bought only the best planes and hired the best pilots and support people. He was living the American dream even though he was financed to the limit. Everything was good until the bottom started to fall out of the market and the crash started.

Tears ran down his cheeks thinking of all he had lost just before the bank called his loans. He walked away with nothing. His home, cottage at the lake, planes, cars, trucks everything was taken. They had been forced to move into a small rental, a dumpy trailer in a trailer park. No matter what he tried or who he talked too there was nothing for work.

What had once been an important date for them turned nightmare for him, they had the same birthday. When he was forty, she was only thirty. Marie was a short, very pretty and vivacious lady that could catch the eye of any man. He had trouble keeping up with her in many ways but he had managed.

Marie had gone back to work in the advertising business. She had landed a job at Starsnick and Benson. Al Starsnick a younger friend of the family had suggested she come to work and the next day she had a job. Her income had kept them going. All he could find was a janitorial job at the church they attended. It paid peanuts in comparison but at least he was working.

Marie started to stay late a few evenings, coming home after 11 and saying they had contracts that were demanding. It only took a few months and Marie started to change and withdrew from him. As time went on the few late nights turned into several. Her attitude towards him became colder and withdrawn. No matter what he tried it would fail, the children began to ask questions, "Where is mom at this time of night, or what time will mom be home daddy? He would only say she was working. He had asked her to call if she was going to be late and that seemed to anger her so he never bothered asking again. Marie had always been a private person and he learned early to never question her.

The night before their birthdays he had left early from work to buy some groceries. He had talked it over with the kids. They would have a big party like the old days. They were so excited. In the morning he had mentioned what day it was and smiled asking her to try and get away early. She only gave him a half smile and said she would try. He rushed home and hung streamers and decorated the house with the children. He had cooked a nice meal and even baked a cake. They were all ready by 6 that night.

By 8 the roast had started to dry out. By 10 the children had eaten and gone to bed with tears in their eyes. At 11 he asked Mrs Bell a neighbour if she would watch the children. He gave a lame excuse about a friend being rushed to the hospital. She had gasped and said, "You go Todd. I will look after the children." He had driven to her office building. The pretty young security guard checked the records and she said, "No Mrs Morris and Mr Starsnick left early according to our records. There is no one left in the building but myself and the cleaners." I am so sorry Mr Morris. The look in her large blue eyes told him the whole story.

It was apparent she noticed his situation as he turned to leave. He stopped and looked back, gave a smile and said. "Thank you Miss, you have been very helpful." He was at a loss as to when the unthinkable suspicions started. The late nights, the excuses all started to resound in his head. The coolness Marie had developed toward him. The words of the guard sounded loudly through his head. "Mrs Morris and Mr Starsnick left early." The parking lot was empty and the cold sweat began to cause him to shiver. He knew the condo where Al lived was a few miles away but he had to check.

He slowed his old truck as he pulled into the parking lot. Al had a ground floor condo. It was the biggest and when you stepped out his south door you were at the pool on the North side of Twin Palms Golf and Country Club. On the East side was his private parking lot. It was then the blood drained from his face. There sat Al's Porsche and the Volvo he had bought her before the crash. It was then he knew the reasons for all the late nights. It was the night he lost his temper and life as he knew it changed. It was the worst night of his life.

Chapter Two

"The Mess He Made"

Todd drove past twice slowly. The anger he was feeling welled up inside of him. He remembered the many times at parties when Marie would have a few drinks to many. Her flirting had caused several fist fights over the years, but she never stopped. He parked the truck and closed his eyes and he revisited all those times over and over again. He could see her with Al working so close to him. Al was a single man, divorced three times because of his own infidelity. Had he done the same with Marie? Maybe if he were to just look he would find them pouring over some job they were working on. Todd gripped the steering wheel of the truck and finally got out and started to walk towards the door.

His suspecting mind had been right. Through the sheer drapes there stood Marie wearing only her skimpy black bra and panties. She was slowly moving her hips to the music inside and Al was sitting on the couch watching his wife gyrating in front of him. What happened next happened in a blur. His size twelve boot was no match for the door. His huge fists were no match for Al. Several swift blows found Al crumpled up in the corner and Marie screaming. He walked slowly toward her and she lashed out a few times at him. All that remained after was hospitals, courtrooms, trials and eventually jail for nearly two years. The charges were many and all felony offences. He never contested anything just stood when the verdict was read aloud. "Guilty as charged, you are to serve 2 years for assault and battery to three people. No less a police officer. Mr Morris that should give you enough time to think of what you have done. Case closed."

Marie and Al sat in the back of the courtroom. They both had signs of being beaten. Al had severe lower jaw damage and Marie a broken nose and a large cut on her upper lip. "Rot in there Todd, you will never see me or the kids again. Rot in there and may you get the same inside." Marie called out.

The judge slammed his gavel and pointed at her. "One more word out of you Miss and you will join your husband. How dare you disrupt my courtroom. Bailiff remove this woman from my courtroom."

The last he saw Marie and Al were being escorted from the court. A smile came across his face, maybe he had gotten in a last word after all.

He had served 19 months in the county jail. His time there was filled with manual work, very physical work. Even though he had been shot and the bullet smashing through the bone in his upper arm he was given no favour. It was here in prison he had again sought forgiveness from God for what he had done. His only peace came through working hard and exercise. His large frame started to show signs of muscle mass. He focused his diet on high protein foods and clearing his mind of the past.

After three months had passed he received two notices. The first was a peace bond to stay clear of Marie and her new man Al. The other was a finalized divorce. That was it he had hit the very bottom of the barrel. He started to use contraband drugs and anything he could get his hands on. He had tried Crack Cocaine once and he was hooked. It was not hard to get it and all you had to do was favours for the inmates. He did laundry and mopped their floors and took their abusive laughter.

He was called to the wardens office early one morning. Bob Riley was a stocky man without a neck. He was big and he was all muscle gone fat, "Today is your lucky day Morris. I have been watching you taking all the taunting and not doing anything to revenge yourself. That tells me that you have some hope. I recommended you for early release. Do you have anything to say?

He looked at Riley, a repulsive looking man with short stubble for hair on his head, large beads of sweat ran down his neck and into his shirt collar. Riley had the most hideous looking bright red pimple on the end of his nose. All he could see was this mans mouth moving slow and his words even slower. Todd was stoned on a large quantity of hash he had just eaten fearing the guards would find it. He caught a few words and held himself as straight as he could and said, "Thanks," he choked back the desire to laugh.

"The boys here have been keeping an eye on you and tell me that you are one of the clean ones. No drugs, no fights and no trouble. The parole hearing was yesterday and you are going home this morning Morris. Thank you for being a model prisoner."

If they only knew his condition that morning. Stupid screws he thought. He smiled again and said, "Thanks."

"You are welcome Todd. Cannot help but wonder what I would have done if I was in your shoes that day. Pack up your stuff and never let me see you in here again. Stay clean and stay sober."

"Thanks," he said again knowing that he better not say anymore. He stood and the guards escorted him back to his cell. He tossed all his things into a garbage bag and stopped and got his pay and clothes and was out the gates within the hour. What now other than to find a place to sleep off this horrible high he was on. He walked a few miles and found a shady spot near a stream and passed out. That was the first day of his freedom.

He awoke several hours later vomiting and with the worse splitting headache he had ever known. He was confused and had no idea where he was. It was a long night nursing his head and aching body. Todd Morris was a free man or so he thought.

Chapter Three

"The Demise"

Four days later he found himself standing in line at a Mission looking for his first meal. All he had eaten was some fruit he had stolen in an orchard late one night. His money he carried was but change in comparison to what he was used to having in his pocket.

The symptoms of his withdrawal from drugs was starting to show. Cold sweats and severe shaking. He needed a hit yet without money at the street value he was lost. His freedom from prison had taken him into a new prison and he was caught inside with no hope of finding a way out.

Inside he stood in line with his tray in hand. His shaking had become so apparent he was not certain he would be able to carry it to the first table without it falling. The last person in the food serving line watched him closely. "Here friend let me help you." He said, "These trays get heavy sometime. Here is a seat for you, mind if I join you in a few minutes I have a break coming anyway?

"Not if you don't mind watching a man eat like a kid."

"Nope I never mind that. See you shortly." He turned and went back to passing out the buns to those coming along the line. He had a soft smile and looked like a kind man. Some of the clients seemed to know him, likely regulars. He had no intention of becoming a regular here but the company would be good. He attempted to eat the meal with a spoon. His shaking hands made it a challenge. He could feel his anger rising in him again after many failed attempts and spilling the food all over the tray.

"Stan Ramsey is the name. Here I brought you another coffee and a few extra buns for the road. Where are you heading my friend?

"Thanks, not really certain. Just trying to rebuild what is left of life. Having some trouble adjusting is all."

"Great if you care to stay around here that is the primary goal of the 4th Street Mission. We are here to help. Tell me Mr, sorry I never caught the name?

"Morris, Todd Morris, good to meet you Stan. It has been a hard few years."

"Hard on many of us Todd. Tell me what is your immediate need. Maybe we can help you get back on your feet?

"The immediate need is a fix as you can tell by the shaking, don't suppose you can help with that problem. It has been four days now?

Stan looked down at his coffee then up at Todd. "Sorry that is the one thing we can not help with but I can certainly put you in contact with people who can. You have four days already, a good start to living clean. We have a small facility up the road with people trained. You look like a man who hates where he finds himself. If you are ready I can fast forward you into the system. They have something there to help wean you off slowly, you interested? From what I can see I would say prison drugs?

He looked at this man and looked down at his food again. "Is it that obvious?

"After you work in this area long enough you see the signs. One arm wrapped around your tray, protecting your food. The way you are looking around and yet not concentrating on any one thing."

Todd sat and again attempted to get the spoon to his mouth. It was shaking so bad he again spilled his food. "Try two hands Todd and move your mouth closer to the food. It worked for me, give it a try. Pay no mind to anyone else. You need to get some food into you."

Todd looked at him and again the anger started to rise. Stan had no intention of making fun of him. He finally took the spoon in both hands and managed a mouth full then another and another. He slipped the two buns in his pocket and stood to leave. "Thanks for the offer Stan, if I decide where can I find you?

"Right here friend. We are open here 24-7. If you need a bed just ring the bell outside. I will be praying for you Todd Morris that you find your way back." He stuck out his hand. "Good to meet you, it will be hard for you over the next several days. The withdrawal symptoms will be getting worse. Your mind will play tricks on you, just know that you are not alone. Come back if they get to bad, you have several days head start, stay clean."

With shaking hand he took his hand. "Thanks for the food and the extra advice and all. I will think about it."

"Good, in the meanwhile Todd, God bless you and keep you safe."

Todd slipped out into the cool air of the night. He had no idea where he was going. He just needed to get away. His mind was fuzzy his gait unsteady and this constant shaking was taking away his energy. Maybe he was going mad, maybe it was the first signs of Alzheimer's starting in on him. He thought of his own father and what that had been like for him. He shuddered at the thought of the way his dad had stared into a world of emptiness. Todd had been there through it all. Marie had refused to go after his dad had stopped to recognize her or the kids but he had gone nearly every day.

He would sit by the hour reading to him. Showing him pictures in his old photo album. There had only been two things that peeked his interest. A full paged picture of his mother Ruth. Her smiling face looking back at his dad would bring tears to his eyes. The stroke his dad had was massive. Confined to a wheelchair with very little use of his hands or legs. His speech had been stolen from him. He had three emotions, tears, frustration and calm. His father was trapped in a world all his own. His frustration would come when he attempted to say something. His calm would come when Todd would read Scripture from the Bible to him.

It was the way he would spend the time with him. Show him pictures and read verses to him. It was were his dad would find some peace from his tormented world.

Todd turned left up a darkened alley. The cold sweats were getting worse. His walking gate was resembling a stumble. His greatest fear was losing touch with reality. All he wanted to do was find a place to lay down. To crawl out of the hell he found himself in. His life was in ruins and he had no one but himself to blame.

Todd managed to find some shelter under the back step of some business. A few flattened out cardboard boxes became his bed. Newspapers became his blanket. His prayer that night was that God would take him from this hell and end his life. He stuffed newspapers under his clothes to help stay warm. Sleep was fitful, the shaking got worse. His memory was fading from the withdrawal. He cried that night for the first time in years. Todd Morris in tears was the start of his new life. He had reached the very bottom of the bottom.

Chapter Three

"Helping Hand"

The sun had just started to light the sky when a door above opened. He looked up and a garbage bag was being dragged across the steel grate above. It ripped open and he was covered in potato peelings and smelly waste. His first response was anger and he called out. "What the hell are you doing for God sakes. Now look at me."

Then came a soft voice. "Sorry I should be more careful. Please come inside and lets see what we can do to get you cleaned up. That was clumsy of me. I should be more careful."

Todd climbed out from under the steps and swept off the peelings and attempted to appear normal. His appearance must have been something. The soft voice again spoke. "Better be careful with all that paper hanging out if you are passing an open flame. You could become a human torch. Here come inside and lets get you some coffee."

He looked up and there stood a lady. She was maybe in her mid forties, mousy blonde hair. Her eyes were sunken, her body was slight but her smile was infectious. "Well what are you waiting for, come inside. I have been awkward all my life. Better get used to it if you are hanging around. Get rid of all that newspaper and come inside, I will leave the door ajar for you. It is the least I can do." She stepped back inside and he looked at himself, newspaper was sticking out all over. Yes he must have looked a sight. He attempted to make himself presentable and tossed the papers into the dumpster.

He slowly opened the door and the smell of cooking oatmeal filled his nostrils. A huge pot was on the stove and his assailant was standing on a stool stirring the steaming mixture. "You take over here and I will get you a coffee. Just keep stirring. The guests get angry if it gets burnt." He walked over and she still stood on the stool. "Better get rid of this," she smiled and reached for the top of his head and removed a long potato peel. "There that looks better. My you are a tall one. I can tell because as you can see I have been vertically challenged all my life. Take over and I will get you a coffee." She stepped down from the stool. She was right she barely reached the middle of his chest. "Get stirring, what are you waiting for?

Feisty little thing he thought and turned to the task of stirring the thick oatmeal. His hands were shaking again when she came back and passed him a cup of steaming coffee. She smiled set the cup down and came back with a straw. "Here this may help. They call me Short Stuff around here. Never once have they been interested in my real name. If you are a gent then someday I may tell you my real name. Better let that coffee cool a little before you try and drink it with a straw." She passed him a damp cloth. "Better clean up a little while you are at it. Keep stirring, I could use some help her this morning, you have made me fall behind." She turned and started to cut fresh bread with a huge knife that was dwarfed in her hands.

He leaned over and took a sip of his coffee from the straw. The strong coffee burnt all the way down. "How long you been straight," she asked with a smile.

"This will be the 5th day."

"It will get harder. Do you have a name. Nope wait I will give you one. Lets see I think Too Tall. Yup that is it Too Tall." He stopped stirring and looked at her. The tenacity of her to call him such a name. Then came the order "Keep stirring, and she again turned to her bread. Yup Too Tall. If you like you can hang around and I will see to it you get some clean clothes in trade for some help. What do you say stranger, that is unless you got something else to do?

"I guess not, looks like I have a new boss. Short Stuff," and he just kept stirring and she smiled.

Just then Stan came around the corner and stopped when he saw him standing there stirring the oatmeal. "I see that you have met our kitchen boss Todd. I see that she has put you to work already?

"Appears so."

"What on earth happened to you, looks like someone dumped garbage all over you?

"Never you mind Stan. Get the bowls and spoons ready. We have company arriving soon. Stop standing around and lend a hand. This place will not run itself. Time I recruited some new help anyway. I see that you are late again. Now get to work before I replace you with this one. I see you have already met but this here is Too Tall." She laughed. "Now get at it and after breakfast you can take him to the clothes supply and maybe get him dressed better than what he is?

Todd stayed in the back and helped with the dishes all under the direction of his newly acquired boss. By the time the morning rush had passed he was close to passing out himself and sat on a chair in the corner shaking violently. "The real name is Mandy Teslin, they call me Short Stuff as a pet name. You look horrible. Here drink this pitcher of orange juice. It will help. Just a few needle marks I see you are a new user. You need some help, Too Tall?

"I do. I thought I could do this on my own but looks like it is taking its toll on me."

"How long you been using? She said and placed her hand on his forehead. "You are burning up man. I better get Stan. Stay here. If you run you will likely die out there. Stay or I will hunt you down like a dog." He reached into his pocket to get a kleenex and found a large piece of newspaper stuffed in there.

He sat looking at it with a shaking hand and blurring vision. The paper was dated from three days ago. It was the want ad section and in bold letters he read "Pilots Needed." He tore off the ad and stuffed it into his wallet.

Stan came around the corner took a look and listened to what Mandy had to say. He bent over and looked at Todd. "So are you ready to get some help now brother. The offer is still open. All I need is a yes and I can get you into a facility that will help the pain?

Todd recalled looking into his eyes and nodding and that was the last he remembered. When he awoke he was in a bed. When he went to lift his hands they would not move. Both his arms and legs were strapped to the bed. A young black attendant came into the room. "Well would you look who has come back from the dead. You my friend have been on one rough trip. Time for some medicine."

He bent and lifted his head up and he drank the fluid. It tasted like orange juice but it had a red tinge and yet had a taste similar to a cough medicine. He coughed at the taste. "What is that stuff?

"It is called Methadone it will help you through the hard times. You have been out of it for three days now. Toxicology reports show that you had Hash and Cocaine and some unknown substance in your system. I have no idea what you been into but better stay away from that in the future."

"That would be over a week ago."

"Trust me what ever it was near killed you. Have no fear you have been flushed completely. Do you think you will behave if I untie you. You were some wild when we brought you in. Sleeping one minute then you took on near everyone here."

"Sorry I do not remember anything after the morning at the Mission."

"Good thing, cause you were a caged animal. If you see any black eyes and bruises just say you are sorry cause they are likely from you. Promise to behave and I will untie you."

He nodded and when he went to sit up he was dizzy.

"Better stay put a few more hours. I will keep an eye on you. Just rest, it is the best thing for you right now."

Chapter Five

"Free Of Hell"

The first three weeks were intense. He found himself
sitting in on many meetings and being coached by several
different councillors. The programs were all Christ
centred and yet each individual was allowed to take his
own beliefs and apply them. His choice was Christ, it had
once been the meaning of life and he knew he would be
needing His grace again to be able to survive.

Over the next three weeks his focus was on owning up
to his mistakes. Accepting all the responsibility and the
blame and forgiving those who had hurt him. The hardest
part was forgiving himself. He was at battle internally with
what had taken place with Marie and the fallout with the
children.

One morning Stan and Mandy came to visit. "Man you
look better than the last time we saw you." Stan smiled.
Mandy never said anything but she only looked and
smiled at him. The visit was short but he did manage to
thank them both. This facility was what he needed right
now and it was what they had opened the door for him to

be free again. "Stan and Mandy I have no idea how I can repay you for what you did. When I get out I would like to come back and help out."

Mandy finally spoke. "Good because I have all your clothes and wallet back at the mission. They suggested I wash them. I did find this in your wallet. Looks like you wanted to save it. Are you some kind of pilot Todd?

"I was at least, I will be looking for work and maybe this is something. I do remember ripping it out of the paper before I blacked out."

"You must be crazy, did you see where this is Todd?

"No, but it is work is all I was thinking about. Not that I was in any kind of condition to be flying at the time."

Stan smiled. "I took the liberty of calling on your behalf. I talked to a man there by the name of Sal Preston of Midway Airlines. He is the owner and says he remembers reading about you in a flight magazine. He says you were a real success story in these parts."

"Maybe years ago, now I could not get a job flying anywhere after what has happened. The industry has its own underground telegraph and once you have failed, well the doors just slam shut all around you. No one wants to hire a loser."

Stan sat with his head hanging and looking at the floor. "What if you stayed clean and sober for the next few months do you think you could fly again?

"That is a long way off. Hard to tell what may happen. Probably if I had something to look forward too I could. Man needs hope you know. A job would be nice."

"Tell you what Sal says if you keep clean and pass a drug test he would hire you."

"You have to be kidding me."

"No his words, I must tell you though there is yet another catch. It is in a very isolated part of Northern Canada. It is a dry town, no booze and they really frown upon the use of any kind of drugs. Might be just the place for you till you get back on your feet. Sorry man just took the liberty of calling."

"No that is fine Stan, I appreciate your doing this for me. Where the heck is this place so I can at least look it up on the map?

"A place called Sachs Harbour. Here I printed off a map from the Internet of North America and it is about as far north as you can go. Summers are short but very warm. Winters are horrible. Sal says he has accommodations there and would be willing to toss them in as part of the offer. Says he is always running out of pilots. They come for a few months then run back to the city. Here is a copy of the email with a list of the planes he has."

He looked at the list then the map and looked at it again. "You are right, the end of the world." The list of planes was impressive but all very old planes. Twin engine Otter, Beaver, Piper Cub, A small Cessna. But the one that caught his eye was an old DC3. It was the plane he trained on fresh out of flight school. Old yes but very reliable. There were very few left.

Stan looked at him. "In the meanwhile I could use another set of hands at the Mission to help out Short Stuff here. The wages are very poor but I have a back room you could bunk out in. Not much but it is a start. What say Todd, think you could get along with this one? He pointed at Mandy. She needs a good helper."

"I have no place else to go. Why not, think you can get along with me Mandy?

"I have had to put up with worse over the years. If you have nothing else Too Tall, you had better take up the offer. You stay clean you hear or it will be me boxing your ears. Do you understand?

"I do, but you might need a stool to get to them." He laughed and before long they were all laughing. "Let me finish off the program. I have another week and with your offer and this one I know I can make it. Never been a quitter and never will be one. I need a new start and this is the best offer I have on the table right now." He looked at the floor, looked up again at them both and smiled. "To be honest it is the only offer I have. Thanks."

"In that case you have the start of a new future Todd Morris. Shall I call Sal and tell him you are interested. He is a Christian man and sounds like he has a heart of gold. First we need to keep you busy here till you are ready for the drug test. That will take a few months to run through your system. Both us have been through it and it takes time and clean living."

"Call him and tell him I accept. Far north or what ever I will be flying again soon. Thanks again for all you have done." Tears began to flow at the thought someone cared for him. Maybe once he got back on his feet he would see his children again. In the meanwhile at least he had hope.

The next few months proved to move slow. His work and the routine of the Mission were always the same. He and Mandy worked well together and he came to appreciate her more and more each day. She shared her experience with him and it had been a hard story to listen too. Her loss was great and yet she had something he wanted and that was joy and a willing heart to serve. He would often find himself sitting with the people who came in and just talking. Much the same as what Stan did with him the first day.

His small room in the back of the Mission became home for him. It was but a temporary stop along the way to his freedom. A place where he felt safe and secure. He had little for personal possessions. He sat late one night looking at what he had. An old battered suitcase, a few changes of clothes and some small items he had collected or been given. In comparison to the old days it was nothing but to him it was his world. A world he was thankful for.

Chapter Six

"New Beginnings"

The crusty voice of Sal Preston spoke into the phone and reverberated through the speaker in Stan's office. "Tell me about all your ratings. What have you got that would interest me to bring you all the way North on my dime or would I need to train you all over again."

Todd cleared his throat. "I have VFR, Night Flying, I have been certified on both single and twin engine. The DC 3 is the plane I certified on. The only thing I would be short of for your flying is a pontoon or ski endorsement but willing to learn if you are willing to take a chance."

"Always something you guys are short of when you want to come North. I can tell you I have taught many and they are gone the minute they get certified. Are you that sort of person?

"Just someone looking for work is all Sal. I have been through the ringer here and there is no work here. All I need is a chance and you will not be sorry."

"Heard all that before as well. Can you get yourself up here on your own or do I need to foot the bill. I have a few connections and can get you up here but man I hate to call in all those favours just to get stiffed again."

"You are offering a place to live right?

"Its warm and that is all I can tell you if that is what you are asking. The rest well I can offer you plenty of hours. Flying here in the North is far different than that easy flying you are used to in the South. If you break down in this country you will likely need to do the repairs in the air. Here you are flying moose meat one day, mail the next then a woman in labour. This is no easy country. A man can do ok if he is willing to live on the edge."

"I guess the call is yours in that case. Tell you what I am a gambling man. I will come up and work a month for free as long as you give me a place to live. At the end of the month if I do not work out then all you need to do is get me back to the next Airport and we call it square."

"I like a man who gambles, especially a man who makes an offer like that. I saw an article in Aviation Monthly a few years back about you. They said you had gambled and made it big." He hesitated. "You have yourself a job. I will get back to you in a few days with a list of connecting flights." There was a pause. "None will be first class but they will get you here. Pack all the warm clothes you have. It is cold here and the winds are coming off the ocean and they go right through you. I will fax all the details down to Stan. Welcome to the North Todd, hope you like what you are getting into. Talk soon."

The phone went dead. "Well looks like you have a new start Todd. Your drug tests all proved negative. I did a little checking on this guy and he is a legend in those parts. Not many have lived through what he has. Are you all ready for this?

"I think so. Warm clothes may be a problem?

"Here," he slid over a piece of paper. "I have a friend with an Army Surplus store on Bailer Street. Go and see Eddy there. I have already called and he said he will get you all suited up. Eddy is an X Addict and knows what you are facing. Says he can put it on a tab for you till you get back on your feet. He is a good man." He hesitated then spoke again. "Eddy is Mandy's X husband. A hard story really so you might want to tread lightly should he ask about her. I know that you two have been getting close so just be careful."

"I will and Stan just so you know. I have no intention of getting involved with Mandy. Just here to help and move on is all. She is a special lady and all but not looking at settling down just yet. I still have a family I need to find. Last I heard I had a peace bond against me so that is hard."

"I know what you are saying. We do need to pay for our pasts and sometimes the past is something we can not change. I did some checking for you with my limited budget. She is nowhere to be found, vanished completely. Her boyfriend and her and the kids moved shortly after you went to prison and the trail just stops right there. Sorry man."

"Stan you have been a good friend. I know I asked about her and the kids awhile back and have all but forgotten about it. Thanks for telling me. I have been praying and I suppose if it is in Gods will then the door will open for them to be a part of my life again. Thanks anyway."

He took the afternoon and stopped in at Eddy's place. The smell of old musty clothes filled his senses the minute he stepped into the dark store. A voice called out from the back. "Be right there just look around."

"Thanks," he called back and started to look at some of the clothes hanging on racks. The full length of the store on the far wall was filled with heavy parkas, insulated coveralls and boots of all sizes. On the other side it was covered in heavy mitts, cooking equipment and lighter clothes. This place was packed and boxes lined the centre isle still to be unpacked.

"So friend what can I do for you? Eddy stopped and looked at him. "You are a big one but I think I can find whatever you are looking for."

"Stan at the Mission sent me. I am heading to the far North in Canada for a flying job and need some warm clothes. It is a prerequisite for the job. What do you recommend?

"Yes, you are Todd, Stan called yesterday and said you would be in. Says you have found the good way of life again and asked if I could help. Eddy is the name and warm clothes is the game. Come to the back, it is where I keep all the big stuff. Tell me how is Mandy doing these days?

Todd heard the warning I the back of his mind again from Stan. "Mandy, not sure I know her?

He laughed. "Short Stuff they call her there. Does all the cooking and keeps the place running."

"Oh yes that girl. As far as I know she is doing well. Never have a chance to really talk with her. A ball of fire though I can tell you and she keeps everyone in line."

"Thats Mandy all right. Now lets see what we have here. Stan tells me you are heading up into the Arctic and these parkas are the best. All left overs from the military, high grade gear this is. Silly to be having a shop like this in the middle of the heat wave in Texas but the young generation are really into this stuff. Lets see I would say that you are an extra large, try this one on."

Todd slipped the coat on and the fit was bulky in comparison to the Texas attire he was used too. Eddy checked the fit, smiled and said. "Maybe a little big but thats fine, give you more room under for layers. Here are a few thermo shirts and some good warm long underwear. Lets get you into some snowpack boots. These are the largest I have." He stopped and explained the order the liners when in and the beauty of the double felt booty, then slipping them into the overshoe. "Never find a warmer boot anywhere. Now lets get you some mitts and some warm headgear. Two of each should be good and I think you are ready."

After they were all finished Eddy took a look at the pile of clothes. Oh here might as well take these and he tossed a large bulky sleeping bag and a huge duffle bag on the counter. Best have it all. "Stan tells me you are good for this. I hear you are starting all over again so tell you what. I get this stuff for pennies on the dollar. Come back and see me when you come to town and buy me a coffee and we will call it square. Always good to see a fellow addict make good. Go out and make us all proud."

"I will, thanks Eddy, you are a good man."

"I have changed, still one thing missing from my life and that is Mandy. Loved that girl the first day I saw her and will love her all the days I have left. I did some terrible things to her and I wish I could have a chance to make it up to her. It was a sad day the day she walked out.

I know where she works and all but can not bring myself to stopping and saying hello again."

"Might be all it takes. Listen to what your heart is telling you. It is a good heart, maybe there is a chance to make up for those years. God bless you friend."

Todd walked slowly back carrying all he had been given, a new spring in his step and duffle bag hoisted high on his shoulder. Tears streamed down his face at the kindness he had been shown by all whom had been placed in his life. "Guide me Father to do the same for others who I find along the way."

Chapter Seven

"Final Days"

"This is for you Todd and what God has in store for you in the North. May he be your co-pilot on all your journeys. He handed him a large envelope. Just a little something from us all. We wanted to make sure you remember us during those long cold nights up there. Keep this card close at hand and when you get lonely look at it and recall our time together and where you found life again."

Applause filled the room. Almost everyone from the Mission staff and the rehab centre had come to send him off. He was overwhelmed having so many gather for him. He stood and spoke briefly and thanked each for planting into his life. "It is often we have people drop into our lives and we are never sure why. The first day I walked in, I was met with love and respect." He looked at Mandy and smiled. "The next morning I had garbage dumped all over me. Who would have ever thought in such a short time I would be blessed with so many good people. Each of you have had a profound impact on me and I thank you all sincerely. What you do here at the Mission and The Centre is something that will never be forgotten. Thank you all and know that you are dearly loved."

As the evening came to a close each person came over and wished him well. Only him and Mandy were left as they finished cleaning up. Mandy wiped all the tables off and he placed chairs ready for the morning meal. "You will not forget us Todd, I mean promise you will come back and say hello again?

"You have my promise Short Stuff. I will be back, I would like to write and send something back for the work here. Mind if I send the mail to you?

"Of course not. I have seen many come and go from here. Some come back and others never do. I think you will be one that will be back. Just a feeling I have."

"I will if God is willing. Mandy I need to tell you I met Eddy the other day and he is a really nice man." Mandy looked down and scrubbed a stubborn stain off the table. He could tell something changed in her.

"Now maybe he has changed but I can tell you when he was using he was not all that kind."

"I understand Mandy but lets realize none of us were who we should have been back then. Do yourself a favour and look him up again." He stopped and placed both his hands on her shoulders. "I can tell when a man is in love and Eddy is a man looking to make a difference. Do it for yourself and please forgive the man for whatever he has done in the past."

Mandy softened, blushed a little and finally spoke. "I was hoping maybe there might be something happening with us Todd. I have grown very fond of you."

"And I with you Mandy but the timing is not right, you know with me starting all over and leaving and all. Give Eddy another chance and we will see what happens while I am gone. Life is too short to be lived in anger and bitterness. Sometimes we need to move on."

"I am going to miss you Too Tall. Is there a chance a girl could get a kiss before you leave?

He took her into his arms and drew her close. Lifted her head an bent to kiss her on the lips. He had to strain to reach her. It was Mandy that started to laugh. "You are right, this could never work, you are just too darn tall. Maybe I had better stay with the shorter guys."

With that said he lifted her onto a chair and kissed her lightly on the lips. "Anything is possible Mandy. Please go and see Eddy and if things do not work out maybe there may be something there for us. Listen to your heart girl and give him another chance."

"You are right, I have been thinking of him a great deal. You know before we got into the drugs we were so happy. We were so in love but then life took over and well from there it was a downhill slide." She jumped off the chair and looked at him. "Thanks for being a gentleman Todd, you could have taken advantage of me very easily. That to me tells me I have a friend with great integrity. Life is going to be good to you my friend.

"I better lock up and get some rest. Stan is taking me to the Fed X hanger at 4 in the morning. Looks like I will be heading north in every winged jalopy in the air till I get there. I have 7 transfers and it will be 5 days before I finally land in that place of isolation."

"Night Todd and God bless you my friend. I will be praying for you each morning while I stir the oatmeal." She turned and walked slowly out the door.

Todd sorted through all his gear again and made sure he had the fax with all the stops and pick ups with him. He sat and opened the card and several bills of cash spilled out on the floor. Again the tears started as he picked it up and counted it. There was close to 700 dollars. He wiped his eyes and read the card signed by each person. Each having words of advice and wisdom they passed onto him. This would be a keepsake which would stay close to him.

He lay down and set his internal clock for 3 am. It was a gift he had and it had never failed him. He was ready to face the world now and he would do so with God in the lead followed by the many who had bid him farewell. He thanked God for all they had done. Yes this had been a good day and tomorrow he would be off on another adventure. In all his years of travel he had never ventured this far North. He had heard much of hardships and now he would be looking at facing the unknown again.

Chapter Eight

"The Edge of the World"

"One last gift for you Todd before you leave. This Bible was passed down to me when I started out again and I would like to give it to you. Just my way of saying that I care for you and want you to have His word with you no matter where you find yourself."

"I can't take this from you Stan. This is yours, something you treasure."

"You can because it is a gift, a gift of hope. My way of telling you that I love you. All I ask is you pass it on to another who finds his or her way in life. In the first page you will see the names and the dates of all the people who have carried this. Be sure and add yours. Best of luck to you Todd and God bless you."

With those few words Stan pulled away from the Fed X terminal in Dallas and turned left on the road back home. Todd stood there for a few minutes, placed the Bible in his pocket and walked into the terminal. In less than an hour they were lifting off on the first leg of the journey. Himself, a pilot and a copilot and a plane filled with crates. This was a no frills flight. Next stop was Oregon. Then onto Vancouver Canada. There he would have a 6 hour layover.

He settled back into the seat and allowed the vibrations of the engines to calm him. It was good to be in the air again. He thought of all the people he had left behind, his family. When would it be before he would ever see them again. Marie had taken care of making sure he would not have anything to do with them.

The captain came back smiled and said sorry for the lack of service but this is the best we can do. Care for a coffee, I have a thermos of black here in my gear?

"Coffee would be good, thanks."

"Great I need some time away from the kid. Questions pouring out of him steady. His first flying job and he takes it serious. So where you off too anyway. Not often we have a stowaway on board. They sorta frown on it, you must be special getting in on this flight."

"If I recall we are all like that when we were younger, you know with the questions?

"I suppose but this one is about driving me crazy, when he is not asking he is talking to himself the whole time repeating all the procedures. The blessing I suppose is should something happen he could fly this thing blindfolded."

"I am heading up to a place called Sachs Harbour in the North West Territories in Canada. I have a few different flights to catch to get there."

"Never heard of it, sounds cold just hearing the name of the place. Do you have work up there if I may ask?

"Flying for a company there. The owner called and made all the arrangements for the travel. I have no idea what I am getting into. From what I hear a gravel runway and some old relics for planes."

"You are a pilot, you know if I was younger I would be heading somewhere North like you. Stay around there a few years and when you come back to the US you will be able to get a job anywhere. That country is hard on pilots from what I hear. Marriage changes everything so it looks like I will be flying this cardboard till I retire."

"This is a big company, the pay should be good and all."

"Fed X has been good to its people. You are right they are big. Maybe one day you will be flying for them."

"Never can tell, sure have seen plenty of changes in the industry. Some like the clients and others like this firm stay with the freight. Some good money to be made once you have established your turf."

"Younger is who they are hiring nowadays. They seem to be willing to work for much less than us older jockeys. Well I suppose I better get back before the kid takes us to Hawaii or something. Good chatting with you, Chuck is the name. Welcome aboard the cracker box."

"Thanks Todd is mine. Thanks for the tips and the ride."

He settled back into his seat. The coffee was hot and tasted good. He opened the Bible and just as Stan had said it had made its rounds. There were 7 names entered and he read each one slowly. Some names carried a great deal of pain and some hard stories about life. The last entry read. *"Stan I know that you are going to be doing some great things. You are a man of God and follow after His heart. Take this Bible and do His will."* It was signed Eddy.

So that was the connection with Stan, Eddy and Mandy. Small world and yet no one had ever said anything.

He read a note that Stan had left for him. *"Now that you have once again found your wings know for certain I will be praying for you. Do His will in your life my friend. Yours in prayer Stan.*

Todd Morris was number 8. He closed the book and slipped into a little rest with the droning of the engines. It was not until they touched down did he wake up.

He rubbed his eyes and looked outside. Portland Oregon Airport looked the same. His next flight was with a small carrier under contract to move freight into Canada for Fed X. Transportation North was the name of the carrier and he was to find a man named Crusty.

He thanked the crew, tossed his duffle bag over his shoulder and walked toward the terminal. Once inside he looked up and down the concourse and asked a Red Cap the directions. He pointed left. "Down there about 300 feet. Knock on the door loud, old Crusty is about half deaf these days."

"Thanks pal and Todd slipped a crisp 5 dollar bill in his hand. Get yourself a coffee and thank God for the small gift, He always provides."

He walked carrying his duffle bag over his shoulder. His size must have been intimidating. The flow of traffic coming his way parted. The sign on the counter read "Transportation North." He went to knock on the door and a lady in the next booth smiled. "Crusty is loading right now. Is your name Todd?

"It is."

"Good in that case he said to just send you in. Here let me get the door. We have to keep them locked. Too many crazies out there." She reached for the key in her pocket and opened the door. When she turned he was right behind her. "Man they made you some big fella. Are you sure you want to see Crusty cause if not you can hang around my counter as long as you like?

"Afraid Crusty is the one but thanks for the invite. He ducked his head and slipped through the door to find a man carrying several small boxes and stacking them in crates near the door.

"About time you got here, must be Todd Morris. Man they make em big in Texas. Come and help me get all this stuff loaded so we can be on our way. Want to ride, you got to earn it Buddy. All those into this crate, pack them tight. Then the rest into that one." Crusty stretched his back muscles. "You look like you can handle that. Need to go empty this fool bladder again. Thanks Buddy, I will be back in a minute or two. Need a coffee I will stop and get some?

"Sure just black is fine, thank you."

Thirty minutes later they were just lifting off the runway. I hear you are a pilot, thats good cause I need to check the freight is secured. Take over, be right back. You still need to trim her. I will set the heading in a minute." He stood and walked through the cramped doorway and left Todd to fly this thing.

The plane had started to dive and he took the controls and pulled back on the yoke. Next he trimmed the plane and before long it was flying straight. That was some gutsy move on the part of this old man.

"Good to see you are not a liar hitching a free ride. At least I know now if I should die you can get be back to the ground and have me buried in one piece rather than several." Crusty studied the charts and punched in some codes, flipped the switch and said, "There now we are on auto, I cheat and have a snooze once in a while when I am alone. This auto thing is the best invention ever. Crusty is the name and I hear you are heading up to Sachs Harbour and working for that old coot Sal?

"Yes I am. Do you know Sal?

"Yup we go back many years. I worked out of that hell hole for six years. Saved every cent I had and bought me this old girl and took on a contract with the big boys. Never looked back again." He spit into a cup that sat in a holder beside him. A stream of brown tobacco hit the cup. "Hard guy sometimes but he has a heart for that country. Hope you can last with him. Best of luck to you Sonny."

Chapter Nine

"Vancouver and North"

The rest of the flight Crusty told him many stories of the north and the adventures he had. "Even delivered a baby at 8000 feet in that old DC 3 he has. My mark should still be on the wall. Just says Baby boy born here."

It had been a learning curve listening to what Crusty talked about. "So where does the name Crusty come from?

"Oh, some old native lady the first day I was flying there looked at my name tag and blurted out Crusty. The name really is Rusty but it stuck, so I became Crusty. Call me what ever you like as long as you call me for breakfast. Need to pee again. Take over the watch, anything happens just switch off the auto pilot and take over."

Then he was gone again. Todd was back into his element again sitting in front of all these gauges. How long had it been since he actually flew a plane. His memory had failed him. Just them Crusty slipped back into his seat. "Here I see that you are drooling so take her over for a spell. Keep the heading on 180. We are about and hour out. Wake me when they start squawking at us on the radio." He crossed his arms and was snoring in no time.

Todd re-trimmed the plane again and check the fuel mix and airspeed and the heading. It felt good to be flying. Off in the distance he could see the lights of a large city. Below the land was dotted with yard lights and some smaller towns. Just then a voice came over the intercom. "Bravo Tango Whiskey 390. Take heading 193 and climb to 7200." He looked for the call signs all over on the dash.

Then the call came again and it was repeated. He woke Crusty up and said, "What are the call signs of this plane?

"BTW 390, just do what they say. Wake me when we touch down. Time you got your feet wet young man. Welcome back to the flying game."

"Bravo Whiskey Tango 390, heading 193 and climb to 7200."

"Good and thank you, we thought Crusty had fallen asleep again."

"No just tied up is all. I am the co-pilot tonight. We are set on 193 degrees and at 7200 now."

"Thank you, see you in a little while."

He looked over at Crusty and he was curled in a small ball on his seat and sleeping like a baby. Crusty was a character he would not soon be forgetting. He switched on the small dash light and checked Crusty's flight plan and the map of the airport. He checked all his instruments and headings and he was right on course.

Next came the instructions for final approach and he started to drop his altitude and airspeed and banked to the left and aligned with the assigned runway. It was a smooth landing and he followed the off ramp to the Fed X terminal and stopped at the signal of the ground crew as he crossed his arms to indicate his postion. He reached over and touched Crusty on the shoulder.

"Time to wake up my friend, we have landed."

He finally stirred "Must have remembered all you were suppose to do I assume. At least I am still alive, never even woke when you landed, you have a good touch. Thanks for the rest Todd. I think its high time I stopped playing this game and retire. Why not stay on here and I can sleep on the way back." He laughed.

"Not ready yet after all you told me of the North. Now I need to see for myself. Great flying with you. I will be sure and say hello to Sal for you. Thanks for the lift and blessing to you."

"Anytime your in the area look me up. Blessings back at you my new co pilot."

Todd finally cleared customs after some questions of his past. The young Border Guard looked official. Todd could tell he was one with a chip on his shoulder and loved the power he had over people. He thought about saying something but just stood and answered the questions. He had a lay over of a few hours and had breakfast and found where he was to catch the next leg of his trip. He would be flying to Calgary, then back up through Northern British Columbia, the Yukon and finally the North West Territories. He would be two more days before landing in Sachs Harbour late on Friday night.

As tired as he was he stayed awake after checking in at the next carrier. He would sleep on this next leg of the journey. He picked up a travel magazine and started to read about Sachs Harbour. The traditional languages spoken were Inuvialuktun and English. Population was 136 people at the most. The traditional name for the area was Ikahuak. Its meaning was "Where you go across to."

It was the main gathering place for supplies for the north for distribution by barge and aircraft. He looked at the map and some of the pictures in the magazine. He looked again and wondered what he had gotten himself into. This looked to be the most barren place he had ever seen. The record freezing temperatures of −70 below were impossible to even fathom.

Todd walked around the airport carrying his duffle bag. It was a sea of people coming and going. Some running others sitting and waiting as he was. He found a small chapel and went inside and sat. He prayed for safe travel and prayed for those he had left behind. It was then he realized he was at peace with himself.

A small man slipped in beside him and smiled. "Taking a break from all the traffic outside?

"Yes and no, I will be caught up in it again soon. How about you?

"Me I am the resident Chaplin here during the day and we are staffed with volunteers in the evening and night hours. Were are you heading off too my friend?

"Starting a new job in the far North as a pilot and just catching the freight shuttles to get there. It has been a long trip but on the final leg now."

"Well Len Atman is the name, from the accent I would say maybe Texas. I have heard many during my years here. Thanks for stopping at the Chapel."

"Right you are. This will be the first time this far north. Glad to have found this quiet place. Just needed to take a little time to pray."

"A good thing. I have been in the Ministry for several years now and I have learned to pray no matter where I am. We have this small Chapel here for people such as yourself to come and rest. Not sure what they have where you are going my friend for Church but know you can pray anywhere. He is always near."

"Amen to that Chaplin. My flight leaves in a few minutes. Thank you for stopping and saying hello. If you think of Todd, please pray for me?

"I will and safe travels to you Todd. Stop in again if you are ever through."

"I will, thanks again and God bless." He reached into his pocket and slipped a fresh 100 dollar bill through the slot on the box by the door. He turned and watched Len as he knelt in prayer. He slowly turned and headed back to the gate where he was to board.

Chapter 10

"Finally Landed"

They had just left Yellowknife and were heading for the final destination. The last three days had been like a reoccurring nightmare of landings and take offs and being jostled from one plane to the next. He was able to catch the odd nap here and there and all he wanted to do was stretch out in the isles of the small aircraft and sleep. They had left Fort Nelson British Columbia at 11 last night. It had only been dark a few hours and the sun was already rising in the East.

He looked around and the small plane. It had three other passengers. Two older ladies and one man. The rest of the plane was filled with three drums of fuel, a whole moose and a few cases of perishable foods. He could hardly sit up straight in this small space let alone stand. The smell of the moose filled the cabin and it was like no one else noticed the animal spread out on the floor.

"Word has it you are the new guy going to work for Sal over in the Harbour? He looked up and saw a man who was he supposed the pilot of the plane. He was dressed in the typical dress of the North. His clothes were soiled, he wore a dirty hat and had not come close to a razor in months. The butt of an unlit cigar tucked into the side of his mouth. He was actually repulsive and he had missed several baths and could be smelled throughout the plane.

"You are right there. First time to the north for me. How about you?

"Runs in the blood this country. You either love it or hate it. You go down in this stuff my friend and you are lost. Might as well kiss your butt goodbye. Only been a few come out of this alive. Your new boss was one. A legend in these parts. He lived forty three days on nothing but water and moss. Tough as nails and about as mean as well. I feel for you, I have seen him go through people as fast as they come. One word of advice, always make sure you have enough cash to get out if you have too. About all I can tell you."

"Sounds promising."

"Welcome to the North my friend. It is the way of life here. It takes little time here to separate the men from the boys. Keep your head on straight and you may make it. Good luck is the best I can do for you." He started back to the front and turned again. "Gus is the name, just taking the odd flight from Yellowknife for Sal, this will be your flight here on in. Glad to be rid of it is all I can say."

Todd sat back again and looked at the passing barren wasteland below. There were no signs of life what so ever, only rock, moss and as far as the eye could see ponds and small lakes and sometimes a river connecting them together. He recalled Pastor Len's words. "You can pray anywhere," and he prayed.

"There she be the big thriving city of Sachs Harbour. Better buckle up folks we are in for a rough one today. The wind is coming in off the ocean sideways. Say your prayers now before I try to land this baby."

There was no doubt this pilot had done this before. Todd looked out the window and the plane was turned far off centre and crabbing badly. At the last minute the pilot pulled up and made another pass. This time he landed with a thud and the plane skipped twice. The landing had been nothing short of spectacular. He would have been a hero at any major airport. Todd took on a new respect for this man. He taxied the plane off to a small building with a revolving light on top. A faded hand painted sign on the outside read "Sachs Harbour Terminal."

The back door opened and there was a flurry of activity as it was unloaded. One Inuit man was cutting off pieces of moose and passing them to people coming with tarps and bags. Before long all that was left of the animal was a front quarter and a red blotch in the gravel where the entire animal had lain. He looked at Todd, smiled a toothless grin and cut off a piece and handed it to him.

The pilot smiled and said, "Better take it, it is a gift for you. These people share in everything."

Todd reached over and took the meat and smiled back. The hunter turned and tossed the remainder of the animal over his shoulder and headed off towards a small grouping of shacks.

"I see you have met the locals," came a voice from behind him. He turned and there stood the man they called Sal. He stood on two crutches. The kind that attached to the upper arm. He reached out a hand. "You must be Todd. Welcome to Sachs Harbour. Look at this you have been given a gift by Nootka. That speaks highly of you already. Well look at it in this way my friend you have supper at least. Follow me and I will show you your place. Only down the road a little ways. Climb in and lets be off before this maniac tries to take off again. This here is my wheels. They won't let me drive anymore so I use this."

The transport was a ATV with a winch and loaded with all sorts of junk in the back. The distance they travelled was short but Sal made sure it was adventurous and showed off his driving skills. They flew past the locals and Sal would honk and wave. Most carrying their newly acquired meat and would smile and wave back.

They pulled up in front of a rundown looking building that was yellow and white and had the name Atco written in black letters. "Northern housing at its finest. Atco trailers are built right here in Canada and have been the mainstay of lodging here for years." Sal said and he got off. "There are a few things inside for furniture and a few pots and pans. It will be enough to get you started anyway. Not sure what kind of condition it is in. The last guy left in a huff. That big blue hanger over there is mine. We start work at 7 in the morning. Just be at the small man door and I will see to it you get some coffee into you at least. What you are carrying there can be your supper.

Welcome to Sachs Harbour." With that he was racing off again and left Todd standing with his knapsack and this bleeding piece of meat in his hand.

He stepped up to the door and found it unlocked. What he found inside was a complete mess. There were empty bottles of whiskey, wine and beer, ashtrays over flowing and a sink full of dirty dishes. The floor looked like it had never been cleaned and what furniture there was was in terrible condition. He stood in shock and wanted to call Sal and demand a new place to live. His spirits were low, this was nothing of what he expected.

The best thing he could do was start cleaning and maybe make something out of this mess and the new life he accepted. He found a few garbage bags in the cupboard and got started. It was well into the late evening when he stood back and looked at his handiwork. He at least had somewhere to sleep for the night.

He walked to the one room off at the end of the trailer and one look at the bed and he elected to sleep on the clean floor. The mattress was filthy and covered in all sorts of stains. For that night he lay on the living room floor using his pack as a pillow and the sleeping bag Eddy had given him. He prayed for God to grant him some rest. He awoke several times during the night to the continuous sound of the furnace cycling off and on.

Chapter 11

"New Day"

It was four o'clock in the morning according to the
clock on the wall. He assumed that was North West
Territories time. The second hand was not moving. He
lifted it off the wall and the battery was all corroded. He
would need to be getting a new one. He had no idea what
time it was. Todd opened the curtains and was greeted by
three Inuit children. "Got any candy Mr? was the
question.

"Sorry kids, no candy, Do you have any idea what time
it is?

The oldest who had spoken to him in English looked at the sun. "Be close to 5 in the morning. We are up early this morning. Do you think we could have all these bottles Mr?

"Help yourself, what are you doing up so early?

"Today is hunting day. The men from the village have been gone for two days by boat. They are hunting Seal and Whale. We are to help when they come in. We will bring you some meat when they get back. We share all we have here."

"Thank you but I have never eaten anything like that?

"Better get used to it mister. There are no cows here. Just what comes from the ocean and what caribou we get. It will be on your doorstep later today. Thanks for the bottles Mr."

"Is there a store here in town to get some supplies?

"French's is the only one. He cost lots of money. Hope you brought some money Mr?

"Call me Todd Morris."

"Morris is a good name. See you later, Morris."

"I will buy some candy and we can trade for some meat. How does that sound?

"The meat is free but if you want we will take candy as a gift."

"Good enough. Then we will trade gifts." They all smiled, each child had the round face he would later learn was indicative of the Inuit. Well at least his first encounter with the locals had been good. First a handful of meat yesterday and today the promise of more needed supplies.

He set his wrist watch to 5:30. It was better to be a little ahead than behind. He trusted the kid's telling of time. He placed a kettle on the stove and looked for some coffee.

All he found was a empty jar that contained some dust of instant coffee. He filled it and the liquid at least turned a little dark. That would have to do for the time being. He would need to do some shopping today.

He stood at the door of the hanger and knocked. There was no answer so he walked to the oceans edge. The seabirds hovered in the slight breeze and landed close to him in hopes of getting a free meal. He looked off in the distance and nothing could be seen. The expanse was overwhelming. They were on the very edge of the Pacific ocean. It was called the Beaufort Sea here. Once in the air he would be able to get a better bearing of where they were.

The sound of a horn caught his attention. Sal had arrived and stood waving at the blue hanger door. He walked up and stepped inside to the familiar smell of aviation fuel. It had been a long while but there it stood, a DC 3 off in the corner. "Stop drooling, that baby is what we are flying in today. We need to make a run over to Yellowknife for our weekly supplies. Its about a two hour flight but I want to get you checked out on her. We will soon learn if you have what it takes to be a pilot here in the north."

"Morning Sal, good to be here."

"We will see once you have been through a winter if you last that long. How was the accommodations. That pig that was there last time likely left a mess. I never got around to getting it cleaned. All the ladies in town are getting ready for the hunt coming back. Happens a few times a year and it is a celebration."

"I gather, I did get the place cleaned up some. Is there a place I can get a mattress or at least a cot in town. The bed that is there is not one I would care to sleep on."

Sal looked at him. "Well it is the best there was for the last guy. You are right, I was looking at it before he came. I have an old army cot in the back. It is yours for the taking. Just toss the old one out at the front and someone will pick it up. Nothing goes to waste in this country. If a cot is not to your liking I will call in an order to sears in Yellowknife. The cots I have are not something a man wants to call getting a good rest on."

"I will pay for the new bed Sal. I need something solid to sleep on. I spent enough time in a cot over the years."

"Good enough, coffee is over in the corner. French's is down the road. They run the place out of their home. Just a garage setup for the basics here. They are expensive but at least they have a few things there." Sal looked out the window. "The locals supply the better part of the fish and seal meat and occasionally a hunter brings over a caribou or a moose from the Territories. Some local trading, they send over whale and seal. Seems to work for them anyway. Me I just fly the stuff. The rest you will need to buy where you can. I have a grocery co-op list on the wall and when I order you can order in under my number. Just keep track of what you order and I can do a payroll deduction."

"Here is all the paperwork we need to fill out. Get a coffee and you can work over on that desk. I will call over to Yellowknife and see if I can get you a decent bed. A friend works at Sears there and always tracks me down something."

Sal got on the phone and he could hear him talking in the background as he filled in all the tax papers. He filled in his Canadian work Visa number so often after a few times he knew it by heart RT612985. He heard Sal laugh in the background. "Oh he is a big one. I would say a king sized bed but that would never fit in that room. I know the one that is in there is a queen. Yeh that will do, toss in the works. Thanks Harry. We will be there in a few hours."

Sal came in just as he was signing the last of the documents. "Stan tells me that you are a good guy. Never met him but he sounded like he knew what he was talking about. Runs some sort of Mission or something?

"He does and yes a good man. They are doing some wonderful things there for people down on their luck. He found the ad I had in my wallet and he made the calls. I will be in his debt for doing that for me."

"Lets see if you think the same in a few months of flying in what some people would call a God forsaken place."

Todd smiled. "There is nothing that is God forsaken Sal. He is all around us no matter where we are He is close at hand."

Sal just looked at him then looked at the paperwork. "We need to get the old girl out and get her ready. You can move the smaller ones out. I have a small forklift and we can hook on with it and pull the 3 out. You watch and I will pull. That way you will see the way I like to do things."

Chapter Twelve

"Rumble and Shaking"

It was like the old days as he climbed into the co-pilots seat and ran through the check list as Sal rattled off the settings on the gauges and dials that were before him. All the pre flight checks were given and Todd repeated them back to Sal with the readings. The last time he had done this had been many years ago. The difference was he was the pilot and his young co-pilot at the time had been the student.

"Very well done Todd. Now radio into Yellowknife and tell them we are taking off, ask if there are any notifications we should be aware of. We have no tower here, we are on the edge of the world as far as Transport Canada is concerned. We are but a fly speck on the map. Yellowknife is our eyes and ears. If there is anything important it is right now, pay attention look both ways before you pull out onto the runway. For all you know someone may be coming in for a landing. Our call sign is there to the right."

"Bravo Bravo Whiskey Whiskey 209 Sachs Harbour, Yellowknife do you copy."

10-4 BBWW 209 we copy, Good morning to you. What did that old buzzard over your way finally pass away?

"Negative Yellowknife, requesting clearance to take off and do you have any instructions."

"You can proceed to runway 19, in case you are wondering it is the only one you have there. Climb to 3000 feet and hold. Have a safe flight and if you are the new guy, well lets just say good luck."

Sal shook his head. "Talking heads thats all they are. Here let me tell them a thing or two." He hesitated then keyed the mike. "You young pups up there in your ivory tower. It is a good thing the rules say no entry at your door or I would show you what a buzzard can do. Cut your chatter or this buzzard may drop a gift on you."

There was the longest silence then came the response. Roger BBWW 209, have a safe flight. See you when you get here."

Sal sat and then smiled. "The door will not stop what I may drop on you. BBWW over and out."

"Shall we Todd, I will take her up and then you can take over." He reached and pushed the throttles forward and the twin engines began to shake the plane. The power that was at hand was evident. Todd sat and watched as Sal moved the plane to the edge of the runway and checked both directions twice. "Always and I mean always check for yourself before pulling out here. One can never tell what is coming unannounced. That is another rule according to Sal."

The plane sat for a minute and Sal applied full throttle. The old DC 3 started to shake and eventually started to move. The sound was like the old days and the plane started to plummet down the runway. After a 100 feet the tail lifted and after another 500 feet they lifted off. There was a new quiet that filled the cockpit as Sal continued to climb. Sal started to call out the altitude "1000, 2000 and 3000."

After each number was called he would call back confirmation. "Ok Hot Shot, lets see what you have. Stay on this heading, play a little if you like get anymore than 30 degrees off course and better call the tower. The talking heads are always watching."

Todd took the controls and the plane dove a little. He slowly corrected it, checked his heading and smiled at Sal. "They are all a little different."

"I know." He called the tower. BBWW 209 we are going to be flying in circles here for a little while. We will be climbing to 10,000 and doing a stall to do some pilot testing. Do we have your blessing. Are we clear to play a little."

"You are BBWW 209. Nothing other than the odd seagull you may encounter, have fun. We will monitor."

"Darn fools, thats what they get paid to do. Ok hot shot lets see you do some sharp turns and climb to 10 thousand. Lets see what you have?

Todd leaned into the controls first to the right, then the left. The plane responded when he gave it more throttle. Sal sat and watched. "Ok lets climb fast and hard and see if you can keep up?

Todd pushed the plane to its limits and they climbed steady. He watched the gauges and the old work horse just dug in deeper and continued its climb. Sal called out loudly. "Geese at 3 o'clock," and when Todd looked Sal killed the engines and all went quiet.

"Now we come to that place in life my friend when we learned what you are all about. You are at 8000 feet and your engines have died. What are you going to do?

Todd reached over and flipped several switches as the alarms started to sound. He continued to flip switches as the plane started to take a nose dive and he watched the altimeter spin out of control. He flipped the ignition switch and the starboard engine fired and caught. He pulled back on the yoke and fired the second engine and it fired and after a few minutes he levelled back to the assigned 3000 feet.

"Not bad. The best part is we did not crash and we are still alive. This is what you call a real life flight simulator. You did well. Consider yourself certified on this baby. Now get us on the ground at Yellowknife. Well done man."

The rest of the flight went smoothly and Sal behaved himself. "I like the call signs for this plane. Easy to remember."

"Should be, I call it Big Bird With Wings 209. Generally that cracks them up at airports away from here. Tried that once in Edmonton Alberta and they did not think it was funny." He laughed. "Just one of those things about the north. Official but we do have some fun."

"Try that in Texas and you would be banned from landing."

"The difference here Todd is we do keep it light. We are all a happy family. Better call the tower and tell them you are 30 minutes out, just passing over Squaw Creek. They will know what you mean."

BBWW 209 coming in due West and passing over Squaw Creek."

10-4 BBWW 209. You are clear for landing on 29. Lets see a good landing. The fire crews are having coffee and they hate to be called. Have a safe landing."

"Tell the boys to bring coffee if we crash."

There was dead silence. "Yup I like your style Todd. Ok its all yours and I will be the co-pilot, its time to run through the landing procedures.

Yellowknife lay off in the West. It was a much larger airport than what he he had seen in the dark the day before. He closed in and and started his final approach to runway 29. "Landing gear down, flaps 20 degrees." He said. Sal repeated and such was the procedure. "Flaps forty degrees," Sal again repeated. "Full throttle for final and back off." Sal repeated again.

Sal spoke out, "100 feet, 75 feet, 50 feet and twenty five. All clear for landing."

Todd carefully set the huge plane down on the runway softly and without hardly a bump. "Touch down and pre check shut down and started calling everything out as he killed switch and turned dials. They taxied up to a trail of waiting cargo carts under the watchful eye of a grounds person signalling. When he crossed his arms in front of him Todd applied the brakes and the groundsman disappeared and he could hear him kicking the stops in under the wheels. "Shut down engine 1 and shut down engine 2, fuel off, ignition off. Main power shut down."

Sal sat back and smiled. "I think you may be a keeper Morris. You handled the old girl like a pro. Do the same on the take off and I will be buying you that mattress. Well done. Now lets get this old girl loaded and get out of Dodge. We have a storm coming in, see that off to the northwest. One of these freak storms that can happen here in the blink of an eye. I would prefer to be in the air than on the ground when I see them."

Sal opened the back door and barked orders at the ground crew. Pallets of fuel, groceries, various cartons and cases and even a few passengers came aboard. Last came the mattress box spring, frame and a box with his name on it and the words extras. He smiled and looked at the sign on the inside wall that Crusty had mentioned. It had faded but he was able to read "Baby boy born here."

45 minutes later, after fuelling they were ready for take off.

"Sal one of the pilots I flew with says to say hello. Old Crusty is his name."

"I remember him. One of the good guys. He stayed on several years. Bet he chewed your ear off all the way."

"That would be him alright, quite the character. I see he left his mark on the wall back there."

"He did, do you have experience delivering babies Morris?

"No, but there is a first time for anything, right."

'Stick around long enough and you will be able to add it to the resume."

Chapter Thirteen

"Homeward Bound"

"She is all yours Captain," Sal spoke through the headset. "Your in the drivers seat now."

They had switched places with Todd on the left this time. He had done all the ground checks with Sal looking on. Now was the moment of truth for him and he was challenged to recall all the procedures. A short prayer and he started and Sal checked him on each. He filed his flight plan with the tower and they were assigned for runway 23.

The old plane rattled and shook as Todd gave it half power and they started moving. He looked at both engines and checked the gauges once more. As they pulled up to the apron on runway 23 he applied the brakes and looked in both directions and called out clear. Sal responded with the word "Clear" and they taxied down to the end of the runway and Todd turned the plane and set the brakes ready for take off.

"Welcome aboard ladies and gentleman, welcome aboard Midway Air and we hope you have a good flight. Sorry Sal here will not be serving dried up peanuts or stale cookies. The best we have to offer is canvas seats and the smell of fuel, dead game. Enjoy your flight."

Sal shut off the intercom and laughed. "They do not understand a word of english. These are from Nunavut, the Alert Bay area. They are coming over for a funeral of Charles Nipsa. Lets get out of here before the storm hits."

He looked off to the West. "I see what you mean about coming in fast. That is one ugly looking cloud."

Todd took one more check and applied full power with the brakes on and the old plane surged forward and held. He released the brakes and it pitched forward. At the 500 foot mark on the runway the tail lifted and at 2500 feet he pulled back on the yoke and the plane started to lift and pitched sideways in a cross wind. Todd corrected it and started to fly slowly upward in a crab right manoeuvre. "BBWW 209 has left the area and heading to Sachs Harbour. Thank you Yellowknife Control."

Big Bird 209 that is a roger, hold your heading and climb to 5200. That should get you above the storm. Nice landing and take off."

"Thank you BBWW 209 over and out. We will be in contact at Sachs Harbour before landing."

Sal sat back and watched while Todd trimmed the aircraft. "Do you have any idea what Big Bird is all about?

"I assume short for BB?

"Right you are but it was taken all the way to be an acronym for the call sign BBWW. Stands for Big Bird With Wings. Smart people from Ottawa that come out here to get their training. Most of them kids and they have nothing better to do. I guess the company colour of white, black and that bright yellow are no help. Sort of stuck."

"Rather becoming I would say." Todd laughed.

"I suppose. We are loaded today. I can feel the old girl lagging a little in this head wind. If we have this at home you will be glad that you have your military gear to keep you warm."

The rest of the flight Sal run through some basics with him. Things he expected of him. "Basically Todd while you are here we are both on call 24-7 up here. No matter what if we are needed we fly. Sometimes we will push the envelope as far as safety but we do it with common sense. If I call on you to fly and you are not comfortable I accept that but I do want you to be ready to go at anytime. That means no drugs, no booze. Do I make myself clear?

"Loud and clear."

"Good because Stan told me you had a problem and I just want to be sure we are on the same page. The first mistake and you are down the road kicking stones. Sachs Harbour is considered what we call a dry town. That means no booze and definitely no drugs.

"Thanks Sal, you would have never known that from what I took out of the trailer. I appreciate you taking a chance on me. Not many would."

"Been there and done all that and care not to do it again. I run a clean operation here and that is the rules. That last guy would just pick his booze up when he was in Yellowknife. It was what got him fired. Glad we understand. By the way the new bed is on me. One of the finest landings and take offs I have seen."

"Thanks I will be obliged to live up to the expectation."

"Tomorrow weather permitting we can try some touch and goes with the pontoons on water. They are both wheeled and pontoon on all of them. In a few weeks the old Beaver will get converted to a wheel ski set up. Are you certified for skis?

"Nope, no snow in Texas."

"Good then I can teach you my way. Take a flip to the right and lets fly in along the coast and see if the hunting party is coming back. It is a sight, this year they took 9 boats and 17 men and boys. They go a few times a year. I hope they had a successful hunt this time. These are special people. They depend on the land and the sea for their food and livelihood. Make a friend here and you have them for life. These people are like family to me."

They flew out over the coast and he turned left and started down the coastal regions. Other than a few large outcropping of rocks it was barren. "Make a turn right and I will show you what is called Arctic Rocks. In the shipping lanes they are known as Death Rocks. They have lost many a ship over the years here. The government is finally going to place some buoys here this year. Ships from all over the world have been eaten up here. Loss of life has been high.

Off in the distance a sight began to appear. A dark brown mass scattered among and outcropping of rocks visible by air. It ran for a thousand feet East and West. Piled among the rock were several large freighter ships and small vessels. Todd banked to the left and circled once. "Wow that is something to see."

"That one with some red paint still left on it was the last one. I managed to land that night and plucked five out of the water. One of the scariest flights I have ever been on. Rough seas and high winds. That is what flying up here takes Todd. A man with skills. Hope you are up for the challenge."

Todd again levelled off and headed South along the coastline. A few miles down a string of small craft were running in a group. The hunting party was coming home.

"Hope you like seal and whale my friend. You get used to it. Looks like they have been successful. Several young men went on this hunt. Initiation from boyhood to manhood. There will be a big party tomorrow night. We are all expected to attend."

"BBWW 209 to Yellowknife, requesting clearance to land at Sachs?

"Roger BBWW 209 you are clear. See you next time up."

They came in for the final and again Todd set the old bird down soft and gentle and taxied to the hanger. The entire community came in various modes of transport to get their supplies. Their two passengers were met with what sounded like a series of grunts. After the plane was unloaded and most of the contents were gone. One of the passengers came over and passed a chuck of meat to both Sal and Todd and bowed slightly.

Sal spoke one word "Nakumi"(Thank You) and bowed back slightly.

The Native man smiled and spoke softly "Ilaaki." (You are welcome)

Todd stood and watched the exchange. "You will learn some of the dialect soon enough. Nakumi is thank you and Ilaaki is you are welcome. These people are kind people Todd. Get the forklift and lets get the rest of this inside. Looks like all the locals got their stuff. The rest of this well that is our work for the next few days. We will use the smaller planes for most of it. The DC 3 is the main workhorse. After we can stuff her back inside. I like to keep her out of the weather. Park the Beaver in last. We will be using her tomorrow. Now that is the real workhorse of the North. Once we are done you are done for the day. We can throw the bed on the buggy and get it to your place. Been a good day Morris. You did well."

Chapter 14

"Town Outing"

Once the bed was inside he dressed again and started walking towards town. The hunting party had arrived and the community was abuzz with excitement. He stood back a distance and watched as the catch was all laid out on the beach. A long rope was stretched out and several people took their places and started to heave to the count of one person in their language. A killer whale surfaced and turned on its back. More people gathered and they all pulled. Quads and dune buggies were hooked on and the pull started again.

A small hand slipped into his. He looked down and it was one of the children from this morning. She pointed and indicated he should help. He smiled and stepped up to the rope between two older ladies. Before long the massive whale was beached. Both the older ladies felt his muscles on his arms and started talking in their native tongue. They pointed at him and then the sky. Before he knew it they were on either side of him giving him a hug.

He bowed, smiled and said "Ilaaki." They both laughed and repeated the word again in their accent and pointed he should try again. He said the word again and they both clapped. He had obviously made two new friends. One ran in small circles with her arms spread out and pointed at the hanger and nodded and pointed at him.

He smiled and did the same and pointed at himself. It was the unspoken word and the actions that identified him as the new pilot. He stood and watched the bee hive of activity as the animals were being butchered. The many young men were all getting congratulated. The older men just stood and beamed with love looking at each of their children.

Todd made his way down the street and again the young girl ran up beside him and took his hand in hers. She pointed at a small faded sign that said French's Store. He followed her inside and she immediately pointed at the many large jars of hard candy. An elderly man stepped in behind the counter. "About all they come for is candy. French is the name and you would be the new pilot. I see they have already met you. I gather you are buying today. Ok Small Wave what is it you like?

"Todd Morris is the name. Small Wave is that her name. It appears as though I have been adopted."

"Buy candy and they will all adopt you. Ok lets see how much do you want to buy mister. Oh lets say 10 of each you have here. Three of them came early this morning and I would like to treat them all. Can you tell her that she needs to share with the other two?

"No need to ask her, you see it is a given here, you know the sharing. Lets see that will be sixty hard candies. Trust me friend they will share with each child in the community. 60 should give them each two. You are far too kind friend?

"Maybe so but children are a gift from above."

French filled a bag with all the treats and the little girl ran towards the door, stopped and came back, looked at the floor and Todd knelt on one knee and looked into her eyes. A small tear filled the corners of her eyes and she reached and gave him a hug and a small kiss on the cheek and ran off to share her bounty.

"I think she is fallen in love with you friend. What can I do for you today?

"I need some basic supplies. Coffee, sugar, flour and some staples like rice and pasta. Mind if I look around a little?

"Help yourself, just call when you are ready. I have the morning shipment in the back. Just stack it all here and we will go through it when you are done."

He had never been much of a cook but he would need to learn quickly. He took a small basket and started to roam the three isles and pick out things he thought he would need. He could tell this would be expensive by the prices. It was a blessing to have the extra cash from his friends. He had done ok in his selection and when French had rang it all through he knew he would be shopping at the co-op that Sal and a few had going on. "That will be 256 dollars. That includes the candies."

Todd tried not to show his surprise. "Minus the 10% for you. That comes to 230.40 dollars. If you you like I can run a tab till you get established?

"Thanks but that will be fine." He counted out the money. It was all in US funds.

"Today I will forget about the exchange rate friend. Let me get this in some boxes for you. Take the quad and the trailer out back and get it all home. Just bring it back when you are done. No charge, just a service for orders like this. Thanks for shopping here, it all helps you know."

"You are welcome French. Count me in as a regular."

"Good, I see the hunt was a success. There will be a party tomorrow. Hope to see you there."

"I should be there. Might as well get out and meet the locals."

They loaded the trailer and he took all his supplies home. He returned the quad and trailer and again stopped at the site with all the game and watched how efficient they were with the tools and how it was a community effort. The children worked like the adults and many waved at him. Todd slowly walked back thinking of just how different this culture was from where he had come from. In Texas all it had been was take, take and take. Here no matter what it appeared it was shared.

His evening was getting his bed set up and the sheets and new pillows in place. The box that had been included had contained pillows and sheets. Sal had gone all out. He cooked his supper. He assumed the meat he had been given the first day was Caribou. It was a pleasant tasting meat. A little on the tough side but he enjoyed it. After doing the dishes he placed all his supplies away. He placed the old bed outside along with the old clock that had long since quit working. He had found a new one in the sale bin at French's. It had all the sounds of wild birds in Canada. At first he enjoyed the sound. Now he knew why it had been on sale. It had kept waking him through the night. As much as he looked he could not find a volume switch. He ended deadening the sound a little by stuffing toilet paper in the grooves where the racket came from.

Chapter Fifteen

"Training Day"

"Those four drums of fuel are heading into Paulatuk to the South. Then that crate is going to Tuktoyaktuk just a little West. That will make a good day for training."

"Right boss, is it that all we are taking?

"It will be plenty for this trip. In a few days we should have all this cleaned out then I think you will be on your own. Lets see how you make out today. Lets get this happening, we have a gathering tonight. This will be a cultural event you will want to be a part of."

It was just after 7 in the morning when Sal radioed Yellowknife and got clearance to do some touch and go's in the area then fly onto their locations. Well here goes have you ever flown a Beaver before?

"No but all looks the same."

"Well lets see how you do. I think I will do the take off this morning. Just sit back and watch. He pushed the throttle ahead and the old plane started to shake and rattle and before long they were heading down the runway. Within a 500 feet Sal pulled back on the yoke and the plane lifted off. "They are known as the workhorse of the North. One of the great things about these is the short take off and landings. You will see some of these strips are very short, you will appreciate the short take offs with this plane. Awesome here in the far north. They are a little slow to respond so keep that in mind when you plan on doing anything. They are as reliable as anything ever flown here. Here you take over and get a feel for her."

He took the yoke and Sal had been right the craft was slow but once the action was started and if there was a need to correct it took a little time to respond. "Keep that in mind when you are dealing with a landing or take off make a mistake and you had better have given yourself a few minutes to get readjusted. Here is the wheel retraction lever. We will be going on pontoons now." He could hear the sound of an electric motor then a clunk, the wheels locked home. "The red light above the words pontoons or wheels tells you where you are at at all times. Make it a practice before you land on either to be sure and check where the indicator is. Head over to the bay over West and lets play a little."

Sal landed and took off several times and explained fanning or flaring the pontoons up slightly on landing. "Take hold of the yoke lightly and feel what I am doing so you get an idea. Just as they were a few feet above the water Sal said now listen and feel close to the way she responds. Come in to far forward and you are in the drink. Think of a parachute and feather your way in."

He could feel the plane touch then settle back a little till they were coasting. "Keep hanging on and feel the lift off, after you can try. I will be right here."

After they lifted off and came around again Sal smiled. "Kill us both and we miss out on a great gathering tonight. Hold your speed and just come down light and slightly back. Thats it, now feel the touch and slowly let off on the power. Just like that man, you are now certified to land on pontoons Lets see you take off."

After they were in the air again Sal slapped him on the shoulder. There you go man you are now endorsed. I will take care of all the paperwork and enter it into your log. Well done. You have a way with planes Todd. Very well done."

The first stop was Paulatuk. It was a small native community. Sal said, "Better tell the locals we are here. Just buzz the town low and lift up again. Remember you are on wheels here." He flipped the lever forward again. They came in hot and banked sharply left and came in again. From this height it was like watching ants coming from all directions.

The landing was again smooth and Sal just smiled as they taxied to a near stop and turned and headed back to what appeared to be the gravelled tarmac.

Fuel was the only drop off here. The unloading was somewhat unethical. Even though Sal walked with crutches there was little that stopped him as he lined up several old tires as a landing place and waved at Todd to roll them out. Several hands caught the barrels and guided them towards the tires. The process only took minutes.

Sal was obviously loved by the locals, children of all ages crowded in and spoke in their own tongue. He was amazed at the way Sal could speak so fluently. When he would make a mistake they would coach him with the right words.

The crowd grew hushed as a elderly lady came forward. Her face was worn dark and wrinkled as leather. She walked with a bad limp and the fingers on her left hand were all missing. A smile came to her eyes first then came the toothless grin. "Nunamiut ganugiq kuluk." (Person of the land, how are you, Love you.)

"Mitta I am well and you are lovely as always. This is my friend Todd." He pointed at him standing in the plane. The elderly woman looked for the longest time.

She pointed at him and smiled. "Nanuq is big one." (Big like Polar Bear) Everyone pointed and they all called out Nanuq, Nanuq Nakumi, Mitta " (Polar Bear, Polar Bear. Thank you Mitta.)

Todd could only bow and smile. "For you my friend, only best from land, Caribou this year. Mitta make for friend. You look after Mitta, Mitta look after you." She leaned in and kissed him on the cheek. "Kulak, my friend, Kulak and always."(Love)

Sal's eyes watered over and he kissed her cheek and took the gift. He reached in his pocket and took out a cigar. Mitta's eyes lit up and she took it and smelled it and patted her heart. "Nakumi my friend." (Thank You)

After all the good byes were said they lifted off again and started making their way to Tuktoyaktuk. Sal was quiet for the first half hour. "Mitta and I crashed one time some 200 miles from here. It was Mitta that saved my life. Her skills and mine allowed us to live many days on the land. If you ever crash here in this country Todd, hope that you have someone like Mitta with you."

"Hope I never do. I heard about your survival out here. I hear that you are a legend in your own time."

"Never something you want to live through. A word of advice Todd if you ever do go down, stay with the plane for 14 days. After that you are on your own. Prepare well for your travel and call on all of your skills to get you back out. The government gives up on you after two weeks. What Mitta and I saw was terrible. I love that old girl. We saved each other really."

"What was that word she spoke to me?

Sal laughed "Nanuq, means Big Polar Bear. Consider yourself as being named. It is a custom around here.

Everyone is named. I need to get you a copy of the book on the Inuit language. I think you need to be studying if you are planning on staying. These people are the kindest of kind. Here try some of this jerky and tell me what you think. There is some smoked Arctic Char here as well. Who says we do not have inflight service on Midway Air."

Chapter Sixteen

"The Gathering and Feast"

It was close to 5 in the afternoon when they landed in Sachs again and it was obvious the gathering had already started with the huge bonfire that was burning in the centre of the village. Long tables had been set up and people were milling all over.

Sal had arrived with a huge smile on his face and a large crock pot of rice. He called it "Wild Man Rice" as it was loaded with Chile Peppers and Tabasco Sauce. Todd was to learn this was a standard offering from his old friend and well received in the community. The festive occasion was one to be relished as the bounty of the sea was celebrated.

Many came over and greeted Sal who in turn introduced him as "Nanuq." It appeared as though the title would be one that was to stick. Todd had children of all ages hanging onto him and sitting on his lap. Small Wave took front and centre attention as she curled in close and held on tight.

"Looks like you have a little friend that has attached herself to you Todd. Not often a man gets that kind of love. What ever it is that has attracted her to you is special to watch."

"Might have something to do with all the candy I bought yesterday, my treat." In any case it is great as he held the child close. "Try this in the south and you would be arrested."

"I know, one of the beauties of living here. The south and its way of seeing things has not hit here yet. Trust is the element that counts. Enjoy the love brother. That is her mom over there, Nitto is so beautiful. She has never married, Small Wave is her child. From the way you are getting looked at I would say she has an eye for you."

"Not ready for anything like that just yet. She is very beautiful though."

"Just saying is all. Nitto is likely the most beautiful lady here in the community. Her quiet resolve has attracted many a man and yet she has remained single. Just saying is all man. Man gets attention like that he wants to be ready."

The food was simple. The standard it seemed was boiled into a broth that had both an oily taste and yet pleasant. There were two large pots. The broth was seasoned with onions and vegetables. It was a white creamy mixture. One was whale and the other seal. He tasted it with some reservation.

He was surprised when he looked up. Her eyes were captivating and her smile was attractive. He was lost for words and only smiled back at her. Nitto reached out with her hand and offered him a piece of raw whale meat. He just stood and looked at it then at her. There was a sudden quiet that fell over the gathering. She stood in front of him and looked into his eyes. Sal had been right she was beautiful. Her eyes though locked onto his were cast down. He took the offering from her hands and tasted it. It was raw, very fatty and yet palitable. He smiled and she bowed and backed away.

"I guess I forgot to mention the culture and customs here before you took the whale blubber. That my friend is a signal that you have been accepted by Nitto. Now according to custom if you offer her some seal meat in return, well that shows you are interested. The next move is up to you."

"Sal, I wish you had said something. Now look at me the centre of attention. I am not ready for any kind of friendship. I mean I have just arrived."

"In that case just do nothing. She has spoken to you. Remember here in the north man is considered king. She will wait for you to respond. Just keep smiling and she will wait."

After what he had been through with Marie and the loss of his children he was in no position to show any affection to anyone, let alone Nitto and or these people. He chose to sit quietly and hold this child in his arms.

After the feast of food came the dance. It was simple, the only instrument was a simple drum beaten by an elder calling out a chant. Sal explained it was a chant of many months of famine and of the bounty that had been bestowed upon them. Each father stood and spoke of his sons conquest of facing the hunt and the spirit that had been given to each. They were called upon and each was brought forward and the fathers blessed each with words of wisdom.

Todd sat and listened and watched each young man receive his right of passage into manhood. Each took on the mantle of the family as a hunter of great achievement. He watched Nitto and the joy that she showed. This obviously was a time of great celebration. "Just so you know Todd the offering of seal meat has no meaning other than the fact you are considering what Nitto has spoken. Not that I am trying to instigate anything but it is a sign for her." Sal smiled and sat back and said no more.

"You are an old romantic Sal, look at you grinning and taking this all in."

"Innocent of anything you are saying, just watching people enjoy the celebration is all."

It was late into the night when the first of many came and indicated that he should dance. The dance was simple, just follow the beat of the drum and dance with abandonment. Finally and elderly lady came and took his hand. Sal just laughed and said "Go for it, anything goes."

Todd stood and accepted and before long was dancing to the light of the fire. Many faces came and went but one that stayed in his mind was Nitto. He watched as she made many moves that spoke of her spirit. She would dance to the left and then the right. The transition of her moves spoke of her inner most feeling. She was average height for these people, her long black raven coloured hair shone in the light of the setting sun and the firelight. Her figure was slight and it was obvious she had cared for herself.

The dancing looked like it was to go on for a long while. Far too long for someone who had to be up early. Sal had already gone home long ago. Todd had been dancing for a few hours and could feel the tension of the day draining. The crowd encouraged him to continue. He stepped back and watched.

Nature had provided for these people just as she had been doing for years. The bounty of the land had been given up to their needs and they had been blessed. He prayed a silent prayer for them. He smiled to himself at the difference life had taken from when he had a family, to the mission and now here standing on this beach with these total strangers. The way of life they had was so foreign from where he had come from. They knew thankfulness and he was a part of this now even though he was new here.

Todd walked over and picked up a small piece of seal meat. The drumming seemed to get quieter as he walked over to Nitto. The crowd seemed to be waiting as she looked at the offering and the man who stood before her. She reached out for his offering and pulled it to her mouth and took the meat from his hands and smiled. She again turned and started to dance with a new abandonment. Her eyes stayed on him while he turned and slowly walked home again. A small hand reached for his and it was Small Wave. He bent and took her into his arms and she whispered the word Kuluk (Love) into his ear. He pulled her in close and spoke Kulak back at her.

Todd was restless all night. He lay and each time that fool clock sounded he would awaken and threaten to toss it outside. His dreams were of crashing in the Arctic and being lost after listening to Sal and the many stories he had heard today.

He awoke at 4 in the morning, made his coffee and opened the door to look at the breaking day. There were two boxes at his doorstep. One with a large piece of whale meat and the other small pieces of seal meat. He had been blessed by the locals. He took the meat inside and carved it into small portions, wrapped it and stuffed it into the freezer. His day had started early and he had already been blessed.

Chapter 17

"Time Passing"

Seasons no matter where he had ever found himself, meant different things to different people. Here was so different as each day meant the need of work to survive. He would watch the boats head out in the morning and see them come back at night with the daily catch from the ocean. No matter the smell of smoke from driftwood would fill the nostrils as it was their way of curing the fish.

Ever so often he would come back from a flight and find a package on his step with food of some sort. Late one evening he was sitting and reading and he heard a sound outside. He looked out the window and could see nothing but when he opened the door he could see Nitto and Small wave walking. He called out and Nitto stopped and Small Wave came running for what was becoming common, her hug.

He looked at the little girl and smiled and then at Nitto and made a motion of drinking from a cup. Nitto approached carefully and slipped off her boots at the door and looked inside. His accommodations were simple but sufficient for his needs. He motioned towards the chair he had been sitting in and Nitto reluctantly sat on the floor beside the chair gathering her child into her arms.

Todd put the kettle on and took a tea bag and showed her and she smiled. "Tea" he said and went about making a pot for them. He turned and she was looking at the book he had been reading. It was one of Jack London's classics "Call of the Wild." Todd smiled and pointed to the book and attempted to make himself look like a wolf. Nitto just smiled. "Wild, Wolf dog," he said.

The sound of the tea kettle whistled and broke the silence, it was welcome. The communication he found was hard. Children were fine but adults were the hard part. He placed three cups on a cookie sheet. It was the only thing he had that resembled a serving tray. He set it down and pointed at the cookies. Small Wave looked at her mom who smiled back at her.

He indicated to Nitto that she should eat and she bowed her head and took a cookie. Silence filled the air and he stood, opened the freezer door and took out a small portion of whale meat and said "Nakumi." (Thanks)

"Nitto smiled. "Ilaala" (Thank You) bowed and smiled. The words seemed to just flow off her tongue smoothly. She had a beautiful voice.

He rubbed his tummy and made a grunting sound to indicate he liked it.

Nitto smiled and said "It is good my friend, better than any food store has to offer, glad you like it."

The shock on his face could tell a story. Nitto could speak english and he was so surprised.

"I should have told you earlier that I speak english. I learned as a student at University of British Columbia where I majored in Marine Biology."

His look on his face must have been worth a laugh. She finally looked at him and smiled and said well at least we have a few things in common. This little girl has fallen for you and we can speak the same language. Welcome to the land of the midnight sun Todd or should I call you Nanuq the Bear?

He smiled. "Now is this not a great surprise. You have me at a disadvantage by speaking english and Inuit."

"The english language is cumbersome in comparison to the Inuit language. Ours is simple and direct. It talks immediately of what needs to be said."

"I am seeing that where one word covers it all."

"It is good that you have come North and helped our friend Sal. He has been with us many years and done much for my people."

"I can see that, Sal is a good man. Tell me about yourself Nitto?

"Nothing to really tell. I came home for hunting season seven years ago after I had written my exams. I ended up pregnant." She hung her head. "It is considered a shame to have a child and and not marry. A long story really but Small Wave is the result and I have been completely blessed and never once looked back."

"Really and you stayed."

"I did, I want my daughter Small Wave to have the best she can. This is where my heart is and not in the south. We do ok and the community has taken it upon themselves to care for us. This is home."

"Truly a place where you have the love and respect of many from what I can see."

"Yes true and without these people close I have nothing. Tell me something Nanuq what brings you here to this of all places. I sense a feeling of loss and yet the spirit roams, lost in time and searching."

He sat for several moments and looked at Small Wave. "I guess it is searching for meaning and coming to grips with loss of family."

"Time heals all, this may be a simple life and yet it is a blessing. Sorry for your loss, death is painful. What you have here is simple. You see we have nothing but love for each other and what we are provided with. Each day is survival."

"No death Nitto, just a hard time and I lost my wife and children to another man. There will be a day when I will find them again. And you Nitto, what about your loss."

"No real loss it was just something that happened. The only thing that truly counts is what I have today, a child born with my love and a child that in turn loves back. The reason I remain." She smiled at Small Wave. "Yours are still with you, here she pointed to his heart. It is where lost love is found. You will find them again."

Todd sat and looked at the child, so innocent of the hardships of the world. The simplicity of a small cookie was all that was needed to show love. How the southern people missed out on much and could learn from this simple act of kindness.

"I see what you mean Nitto. You are doing well. I mean alone and all."

"We do live day to day here. When we have nothing, we have everything. Look at this child and tell me I need more. What I have is all that I need."

Their short time they had together left him to understand what Nitto was talking about. She had all she needed, he would find what was his again someday. In the meanwhile what more could he ask for. "I do need to get this girl home. Thank you for the tea and your company Nanuq." She stayed only a short time before she said goodbye.

His thoughts the remainder of the night were filled with the frustration of what he had left in the south. They were soon replaced with the meaning of what Nitto had said of living here. He had finally found a place where he found some peace. His surroundings were meagre and yet fulfilling. He had no idea how long he would be here and yet he knew this was where he belonged for the moment.

The close of his day was like many. Looking at the card of well wishes he had of the friends in the south. They meant well with what they had said and yet did they really understand the true meaning of life. This place had changed him and he was beginning to like the change within himself where he had come to set aside wealth. Could he be happy here in this barren land.

Chapter 18

"Flying Hunt"

Sal had certainly trusted him with missions of flying alone. He would be given the line up for the day and Sal just left him to himself. The only time Sal would be with him was on the Yellowknife runs with the DC 3. "Never mind me, I just need to travel with you. I love this old girl and she has never left me alone or me left her alone."

"Great to have the company. Starting to get colder now. I see the locals are gearing up for some hunts."

"They are. The next one is for Caribou. Have you ever hunted Todd?

"A little when I was a kid. Dad would take me along. About all it ever turned out to be was a big drunk with a few of his buddies."

"I have a flight booked for next week. Five local hunters heading over to the caribou grounds in the Territories. It would be a good time for you to do some hunting. Maybe bring a few home for us. I used to go but this leg is giving out on me."

"I do not even have a gun or licence."

"You can use mine and use my tags I bought. I have already registered you as a proxy hunter for me. Being handicapped has some advantages." He laughed and said, "See that way you can do all the work. The bonus is I get to do all the eating. Have no fear I will see too it you have plenty of meat. Way ahead of you Pal."

"I have lots of food Sal. The little freezer I have in the top of the fridge is full."

"There is a deepfreeze in the back of the hanger. Just put what you want in there. I hear you have been getting a few special donations by some pretty young lady and her daughter. Looks to me like you are being accepted as one of the hunters. Time you proved yourself with this hunt and returned some of the blessings back to her." Sal laughed. "Looks to me like maybe someone has taken you seriously Todd, that is a good thing my friend."

It was only 4 in the morning when he started the Beaver and his passengers started to arrive. The conversation was very limited as only one knew enough english to instruct him where to go. At 4:22 am they lifted off and after a few hours came across a site not many men would see. The Porcupine Caribou herd was on the move. Mile after mile of animals travelling south after their summer in the tundra and calving season. The chatter started in the back of the plane. Gritlo, the english speaking man came forward and pointed at a lake off to the west. There, we hunt."

Todd banked the plane and came in for a landing and taxied to the shoreline. The men were already jumping out into the freezing water. Their clothes and seal skin boots kept them dry. Gritlo tied a rope to the strut of the pontoon and pulled the plane to shore. They tied it front and back. Gritlo whistled and all the men gathered and he explained the hunt by scratching their route with a pebble on a large stone. They would split up, two men per team and skirt out wide enough to maximize the hunt. Gritlo pointed to the first two men and the direction they would go. Next to the other two and their direction. He turned and looked at Todd. "We go here," he pointed off straight ahead. "No shoot till men shoot." He pointed at the first two men that had been dispatched. They were already on a slow run and crouching low.

Gritlo moved with ease through the slippery tundra. Todd had trouble, his boots were slipping all over. Gritlo stopped and smiled. "Move with light feet." He showed him what he meant and it worked better. It made all the difference as he bent and followed this man. They found a high vantage point and lay quiet. The caribou were passing steady and only a few hundred yards away. It was a wall of animals. Who could miss a shot at so many animals gathered like this.

Gritlo looked to the left and then to the right. All men had taken their places. He gave a signal and the first two stood and each fired all three of their shots. He signalled the others and they did the same.

The animals that were right in front of them stopped and were milling around in fear. "Now Nanuq we take biggest only, take time to look. Big horns, big animal. They stay laying and Gritlo carefully took aim and the rifle jumped and a great bull fell to the ground. Todd picked a caribou with a massive rack and one shot and it fell. Two more shots and Gritlo sat up. Todd took aim and dropped two more animals.

They stood and started to walk towards the passing animals and they all shifted to the east and ran a mile before they again formed a line and kept moving. In total they had 18 animals on the ground. Not one shot had missed its mark. Each man had taken his allotted animals.

The men on either side started the task of field dressing their animals. Gritlo pointed to he three largest animals and the tags he carried. "You mark yours, Government says. Me I am free to hunt."

He had only watched his dad do this once. Gritlo smiled and tapped him on the chest. "You, me work together, you watch first." He bent and slit the throats of all their animals first. Blood poured out onto the land.

He watched as this man made short work of the first. He stood back and pointed at the next and smiled. "Now you."

Todd did the same and occasionally Gritlo would stop him and explain a better way. After his was done his friend dipped his finger in the blood and drew a line on Todd's forehead. "Nanuq now hunter, he took a slice off the liver and ate it raw and cut a piece for Todd and passed it to him. He looked at Gritlo then at the meat and finally slipped it into his mouth. He smiled "Good." He was actually surprised at the flavour, still warm from the animal.

Gritlo smiled and carried on with the work at hand. It was getting late by the time they dragged all the animals back to the plane. "Gritlo and men stay tonight, you take meat back to Sachs. Come back when done."

"You have no tent and it will be cold."

"For you yes, this is my tent friend and he pointed at the sky. We be fine. You go now and come back. Have people at Sachs help. Fly low and they come. You good hunter my friend. Now you go."

He did a quick estimate of the weight in the plane. It would be close to 5000 pounds. He would be a while getting off the water with that much weight. He started the plane and taxied to the far end of the lake and turned the nose into the wind and gunned the engine to full throttle. The Beaver lumbered along slowly gaining speed. The far shore was fast approaching he held off till the very last minute and pulled back on the yoke. He lifted off at the last possible moment, banked and flew back over the men. They already had a fire built and stood waving.

It was 9:02 pm exactly when he made a long low pass over town. He turned and came back over again and there were already several quads and trailers heading to the strip. Sal came out and smiled when he opened the door. "What did you take the whole herd?

"Just the easy one Sal. Your tags are filled man."

"You mean to say that you shot three animals yourself. Well I will be, that is awesome. One is all yours. I will share mine with the others. Well done."

"Thanks Sal. I will be sharing mine as well. After we get this unloaded I will be heading back right away to get the men."

There was a buzz of activity around the plane. I will hang yours in the hanger for you. It will be nice and cool there. I will get it skinned."

"I will skin the animal Sal came a soft voice." It was Nitto. "It would be an honour to help this fine hunter with his game. I see you have been marked as a hunter." She pointed at his forehead. "Considered to be a great honour you know."

Sal cleared his throat. "Sure Nitto. I will get it inside for you." He walked slowly away and got his dune buggy. The rest of the animals were taken and loaded. Two hunters helped Sal get theirs inside and hanging. Todd stood smiling, Nitto turned once and smiled and waved.

He waved back and she turned taking Small Wave by the hand. She had a task to take care of."

It was near midnight when he touched down again with the hunting party. He pulled up to the wash bay and started to wash the inside of the plane and all the men got in and helped scrub things down. He was amazed at these people and their willingness to work together. He stood and waved at them as they headed back to their homes. They chatted and pointed at Todd. "Good Nanuq."

Todd was tired and after he checked the meat he stepped into his small trailer and found a pot of stew on the counter and a note. All it had was a smiley face on it. He grinned and sat and ate, it had been another good day in the North.

Chapter 19

"Taking Time"

The following week he decided to butcher his animal. He had gone to French's and bought some wrapping paper, tape and a large knife, a saw and a sharpening stick. He had just opened the door when Nitto and Small Wave came in. "You look like a man on a mission with all that gear? Her smile was warm and friendly. He gave French a dollar and said, "For my little friend here. I know she is sweet but a little more will never do any harm."

"You are too kind Nanuq, you have many friends here in the community. People have spoken highly of you. Good hunter, they are saying you will make a good Inuit man someday. It pleases Small Wave and I too watch you and the people. The last man who was here was a horrible man and everyone here hated him."

"Well that is good news. Nitto I want you to have some of this caribou that I shot. It will be far to much for me." He bent over and looked at Small Wave. "I bet that you really like caribou almost as much as you like candy?

She said something and Nitto translated. "Candy is better but I like stew."

He laughed. "So do I, it was a staple as a child on stew. It was my favorite meal. Your Mom cooked a great stew the other night."

Her mother explained it to her. Then Small Wave took his hand and started to pull him to the door. "What is it child, where are you taking me? Small Wave stopped and said a few words to her mother then Nitto blushed. "She thinks you should come for some stew to our house?

He bent and took her into his arms. "So that is what you would like." He stumbled with the word but said "Nakumi."(Thank You)

Small Wave's eyes lit up and she hugged him. "Ilaaki." (Your welcome)

I had better see if I can cut up this caribou tonight. Never done anything like this before."

"We can have the promised meal some evening soon. Let me drop Small Wave at her grandmothers and we will butcher together."

"Are you sure Nitto you skinned the animal. The meat was to pay you back for all the work?

"Four hands work faster than two.

He still held Small Wave and her mother told her what was happening and she clapped her hands together and kissed him on the cheek. "Come and meet Small Wave's grandmother then we will go to work." They walked through the small hamlet towards a very tiny shack near the ocean. Small Wave had a hand in each of theirs and all she did was smile and skip along.

"I hope this will not cause a rumour in the community for you Nitto. I mean me walking with you and all."

"It is fine, the rumour has been started when I gave you some whale and you gave me some seal meat. It is tradition you know meaning that we are interested in each other. It is our way Todd. There will be no rumours other than the ones going on now."

"I see, well that is news to me, other than what Sal told me the night of the celebration. You know the tradition and all. I was not aware of it until after you have treated me with the whale."

"I can assume in that case then you have accepted my offer of wanting to get to know you better. I mean you gave me the seal knowing what it means?

"Yes Nitto, very much interested."

"You really do need to spend a little more time around here Nanuq. You are missing all the news. She laughed as she knocked on the door of the cabin.

"Nanapi," and she pointed at him. "Nanuq," then went into a long conversation with the lady in Inuit.

Nanapi was short very robust and Todd assumed she must be well into her eighties. She reached out and touched his upper arm and smiled. Tapped him on the chest a few times. "Meta Nanuq, Meta." (Big Polar Bear, big)

Small Wave slipped into the cabin and Nitto explained in their language they were going to cut up an animal. Nanapi smiled and nodded in his direction. He smiled back and told Nitto to tell her that he would send some meat back for her. After Nitto told her she moved in close and gave him a hug. Her head was hardly to his belly button. "Meta Nanuq" and she stood back and smiled. They stopped back at French's and got a few small boxes from the back of the store and walked slowly to his trailer. "I will make us a thermos of tea for while we work."

"Thanks, I will get started on the caribou. Give me all this stuff. I left a knife here the other day. Thank you for caring so much for Small Wave. She has never had anyone to look up too. Thank you Todd."

"You are welcome. See you there in a minute or two."

When he got there she was already splitting the animal in half it's full length down its backbone working with an axe and her knife. "This is the first thing you do, from there we need to lay it out on some sort of table and can break it down further into proper cuts." She looked around the hanger. "There are two sawhorses, now all we need is some plywood or something?

"I saw some over in the next bay the other day." He set up the sawhorses and set the plywood in place. Nitto unrolled the paper and taped it down with the waxed side up. "There we are ready. Can you set half down on the table. Nice and clean. This is good."

Todd lifted the half and easily lay it down. Nitto made several marks with her knife and explained the way it would be cut up and in a few minutes had it broken down in three pieces and pointed to each. "Front quarter, ribs and hind quarter. Some is roasts and stew in the front, the ribs make good eating anytime and the hind is where we find steaks and roasts. I will cut this half and you do the woman's work and wrap. You can do the next." She got a little glint in her eye. Here men do both jobs."

As a child he was a wrapper for the family when it came to butchering. Nitto just watched the first package of meat getting wrapped. "Very well done, you have done this before I can see?

"I have years ago when I was a child. Looking at you handling that knife I would say that you have some experience butchering as well?

"It is our way, I so appreciate watching the community come together for the common good of all. It is just as God calls us to be and I can see that you will fit in here just fine." She looked down at her work again. "That is if you are planning on staying."

It was not a question more a comment she made and yet he felt the need to answer. "For now this is my home. It is all I have and the more time I spend here in this land and with the people the more I understand the way it should be lived."

"That is a good thing. Keep wrapping you are falling behind Nanuq." She looked at him and smiled. "It is good that you have found a home here." They finished the first half then she smiled. "Time to trade places come get this other half on the table and I will guide you and wrap. The caribou will be a blessing for all who eat it. Some of the finest meat I have seen in a long while. You are a good hunter Nanuq and a good man."

It was a few hours later and they had all the meat cut, placed in Sal's deep freeze and everything cleaned up. "We forgot all about our tea, care to come to the house and get washed up and warmed up. It is cold in here. I will bring the meat to you tomorrow, time to get you warmed. Thank you for all the help."

Chapter Twenty

"The Tea Visit"

She stepped into the small trailer and slipped off her coat washed her hands in the sink. Todd could not help but notice how slim she was. Her long jet black hair reached past her waist. It was shiny and full. He reached over and took a clean towel from the cupboard. She turned and bumped into him. Time stood still and he took her into his arms and kissed her softly on the lips. "You are the most beautiful lady I have ever seen Nitto. She looked at him as he dried her hands then tears started to fall down her cheeks. "I am sorry Nitto I should not have kissed you."

"No silly its not that you kissed me." She wiped the tears from her eyes. "It is the fact that you did kiss me. It is something which has not happened in a long while. Thank you Todd."

She slipped into his arms and pulled herself close to him. Her head barely reached the middle of his chest.

The smell of her shampoo reached his nostrils and he took a deep breath. "You are more than welcome. Thank you for being such a wonderful mom and a great helper with everything. I guess now the rumours are official. You know that we are an item?

She looked up at him and smiled. "Like I said Nanuq you have been living in the dark for the past while. That little piece of seal meat pretty much made the announcement that I was taken. Please lets move slowly and take our time. I have only been with one man and I made a promise that I would remain pure. I have been true to that commitment. I hope you understand?

"I do and I will be more careful in the future. Thank you for caring for a lost stranger the way you have. I was a lucky man the day Small Wave came into my life. After all look what she brought with her. We had better have that tea now."

"Quickly, I do have to get Small Wave and get her home to bed. Grandmother will have fed her and spoiled her by now."

"In that case I will slip over to the hanger and get a gift for Nanapi, what do you think she would like?

"What ever you wish to give her. What you give is to come from the heart and that is where she will see it come from as well. Small or large Todd, it is all the same to these people."

"Sit and have your tea. I will be right back." He slipped on his boots and parka and walked to the hanger and filled a smaller box with an assortment of meat. He stood and looked at it again and added a few packages of ribs. When he walked back into his home he found her looking at his card.

"I am sorry I should not be looking at your things."

"I have nothing to hide and he laughed, just some old friends who wanted to see me off in style and say goodbye. The card is signed by them all."

"They must have cared a great deal for you from all the comments. That speaks highly of you and the kind of man you are. Thank you for allowing me to have a look at this. It is awesome that you have such true friends."

"All ready," he helped her with her parka and opened the door. The night wind had started to blow and the cold air coming off the ocean was brisk. She slipped her arm into his and cuddled in on the opposite side of him.

"You are big enough to make a good windbreak Nanuq," She looked up at him and laughed. A few minutes later they knocked at Nanapi's door and Small Wave came running. She was happy to see them. He ducked as he stepped into the small cabin. The doorframe was shorter than normal. He kicked off his boots and set the box of meat on the counter. Nanapi looked and held her hand over her heart. She smiled and looked at him and took his hand and studied it. She raised a hand as if to say wait. She made her way through piles of boxes and tables with crafts all over. A few minutes later she came back and handed him a pair of hand crafted leather mitts.

Todd stood looking at them. The beadwork and stitching were exquisite. They were made with seal fur and trimmed with white Arctic Fox fur. He looked up at Nanapi and reached into his pocket for some money. She closed his hand and pointed to the box then the gloves and took his hand and shook it.

"I think you have just made a trade Todd. You will never have cold hands as long as you have those with you. Slip your hand inside and you will see why."

He pulled on one of the mitts and instantly his hand warmed. He looked inside the other and it was completely lined with the white Arctic Fox fur. He pulled off the mitt and looked at them and reached for Nanapi and gave her a hug and kissed her forehead. "Nakumi Nanapi."

She bowed slightly and said "Thank you," in english.

He walked Nitto and Small Wave home. Small Wave had climbed up into his arms and was sound asleep as they walked. A fresh snow was falling and it crunched under their feet in the cold air. Nitto opened the door and motioned for him to carry Small Wave into her small bedroom. They both worked at getting her out of her parka, mitts and boots. Nitto covered her and they walked to the entryway again. "Tomorrow you will come for the stew I promised. Come when ever you like. Small Wave and I will start it early. Thank you for the evening. I enjoyed spending time with you."

"And I with you. I will bring you the meat as well when I come."

She stepped in close took his face into her hands and stretched on her tip toes and kissed him softly on the lips. "Thank you for being a gentleman tonight. You are a kind man."

"You are a lovely lady. Thank you for offering me whale meat. It is the best thing that has happened to me since I arrived. I think you can safely say I will be staying on here. I have started to really like the countryside." He smiled at her. "The company is a bonus."

"Good night Nanuq. Enjoy the walk home and enjoy the mitts. They are the finest in the land. Rest well my friend. Rest well."

He slipped out the door and started to walk home. He pulled the hood of his parka over his head and walked towards the ocean. Cold could not stop him from enjoying the night. He walked a few miles before he turned and started for home. He whispered the word "Home, yes I have found home."

Chapter Twenty One

"Extra Flights"

On the last flight to Yellowknife the starboard engine on the DC 3 started to act up about an hour out of the airport as they were heading home. It would fire then cough black smoke and die again. Sal had gone to the side windows and when he came back he said. "I think we have a jug or cylinder wall that has gone. We can make it back on the one engine. Best not try and start this one again."

"I recall seeing one of those taken apart years ago in Texas. Four bolts and you change it out."

"True as long as that is all that is broken. Sometimes the piston flies apart inside and you end up with a big repair bill. If it is just a jug then it is simple. The hard task is finding a jug for this old girl. Best throttle her back a little and give the good engine less of a load."

Once they landed and dealt with all the cargo Sal and him took off the cowling and looked at a gapping hole in the side of number 6 jug. Once pulled off they could not see any damage. Sal got on the phone and made some calls. He was unable to find any through his regular leads. He placed another call to Tundra Air out of Whitehorse in the Yukon. "Heh, Lefty its Sal up here in Sachs. I need a jug for my old girl. Would you have one you would be willing to part with?

"You old bandit, are you still limping along with that old stuff. You must be one of the last. Maybe time you gave it up and stuck it in a museum somewhere. Let me have a look. I sold all mine but I found several boxes of older parts again the other day. I will call you in a few minutes."

Sal hung up the phone and stood smiling. "May have hit the Gold mine with Lefty. We go back many years he and I, tell you what if he has something I will send you down to Whitehorse to get the parts. Give you a chance to get some civilization into you."

"What ever you need boss, consider it done." The phone rang again. It was Lefty and Sal gave him a thumbs up.

"That is great Lefty. I will send my man down tomorrow. Today is Friday right, are you around over the weekend. He wrote down a number?

"Should be, not planning anything."

Consider it all sold, just let me know what you want for it all. Thanks Lefty."

"Looks like you are going on a trip Todd. Seeing as how it is normally your days off tell you what. Why not take Nitto with you and you can have dinner and have a good time on old Sal here. You been working hard and maybe its time I gave you a bonus. Here take the company credit card and enjoy yourselves."

"Mighty kind of you Sal. He reached and picked up the card. Are you sure I mean this could cost you a small fortune, you know feeding me and all?

"Positive but I think you should ask Nitto to go with you. From what I hear you two have been seeing a fair amount of each other. Time maybe she saw you in a different light." He stopped for a minute. "Better get two rooms young man, no hanky panky happening with that girl, you hear me?

"I hear you Sal, thanks for the warning. I will slip over and see her this evening and see what she says. They have asked me over for dinner. I guess we are done for the day."

"We are, good to know we made it back in one piece. Now go and have a good evening."

Todd slipped on his parka, boots and mitts and pulled the hood over his head and started to head over towards Nitto's place. He had started to wear a regular path down from his small home. His knock on the door was answered, "Come in please."

He stepped into her small home, slipped off his boots and parka. "Care to come on a date with me Nitto. I have to make a trip over to Whitehorse in the Yukon tomorrow. Sal suggested you come along and we both get a little culture into us. Love to have you come along. Sal says stay over if we like." He hesitated and added. "Two separate rooms of course."

"What about Small Wave?

"Good point, we could bring her along but with the cold weather and all maybe a good idea she stays with Nanapi. Would that create a problem?

"No of course not. Nanapi will be more than happy to have her to herself. Sure it would be ok. I will call her now." She stood and on the way by kissed him on the cheek. "You and I on a date in the big city. That is special of Sal. He is an old romantic at heart." She spoke in Inuit to Nanapi and turned and blushed. "She says it is ok as long as you behave yourself." He raised his hands in the air. She turned back to the phone and laughed and spoke a few words then hung up. "This is very exciting Nanuq. Our first real date in a new city. I would be honoured to come along."

They sat and had supper and Small Wave sat staring at hime. Each time he looked at her shy blushed. Nitto just smiled. "You do have a way with the girls Todd."

"Not really, she is a beautiful child Nitto. You have done well all by yourself and raising her and all."

"It was getting late, I should be off here. Thanks for the wonderful dinner, meet you at 7 in the morning at my place. Pack all your warm clothes and a few supplies. I will pack some food as well and a rifle. We will take the twin engine Cessna this time. We will travel in style. It is well equipped with plenty of safety features. See you at 7 in the morning."

"See you then she leaned in and gave him a hug. Thank you Todd Morris. This will be great. Now I am all excited. Shall I pack something fancy for dinner. I do have some nice clothes that I have not worn in years."

"Please and anything we do not have, well I have Sal's credit card."

"See you then. I have just the dress in mind. This is so exciting Todd."

It was 6:30 when the knock came on the door. He called out come in and she stepped into the small trailer dressed in tight jeans and a new parka he had never seen. Her hair was combed off to one side and she looked amazing. "Oh my look at you Nitto, you are beautiful."

She set a small suitcase on the floor, smiled and said, "And look at you, clean shaven and dressed in your best. We will be flying in style."

The Cessna was a beautiful plane to fly and luxurious compared to anything else Sal had on his fleet. "Its what I call my toy he said. Won the thing in a poker game years ago. That is a long story. Have a safe flight you two and enjoy yourselves is all I can say. See you when you get back." The flight down was uneventful other than a storm blowing in from the West. The terrain started to change an hour out from Sachs and off in the far distance the mountain ranges could be seen. It was his first time in the daylight hours in Whitehorse and they flew a few circuits around the city. It was shortly after four in the afternoon when they landed. The first order of business was to call Lefty.

"Good you called I was just locking up shop. I have all the parts right here. I found two jugs so that should keep that old bandit out of trouble for a spell. The rest tell him I just tossed in. I will send a bill later. Might as well store your plane inside tonight. The code for the door is 6429. Just lock her up when you leave. Heading out tomorrow to do some ice fishing with the old boys."

He parked the plane inside. They called for a cab and found two rooms at the newest hotel in town. He helped

Nitto with her luggage and she pushed him out the door. "A lady will need a few hours to get ready, so go do what ever you guys need to do. I will call you on your extension when I am ready. The lady at the desk says this place is as good as anyplace in town to eat. See you later Nanuq," as she pushed the door shut.

Chapter Twenty Two

"The Longest Date"

Nitto phoned his room. "I am as ready as I will ever be. Care to come and get a lady and take her out."

After the first knock the door to her room opened and Todd stood with his mouth hanging open. "Look at you," was all he could say. Nitto had chosen a small white dress with a row of flowers at the hem. It accented her figure and her long hair was curled and shaped around her face. Her earrings and necklace highlighted her features. "Nitto you are beautiful, I do appreciate this look."

"Glad you approve, shall we," she said and pulled her door shut. "You are looking rather dandy yourself you know."

"Nothing in comparison to you," he said leading the way to the elevator. "I have a table reserved for us in the dining room, then we are off to see a live theatre they have here in the ballroom called the Frantic Follies. They say it is something you have to see."

"Sounds wonderful. Thank you for bringing me along on this trip. I do miss the city life when it comes to doing things like this. No place to dress up for where we come from." She laughed as they stepped from the elevator. "I do think I would be out of place if I wore this at home." Heads turned when they walked into the dining room.

"They are looking at you Nitto, not me." He smiled and the hostess took them to their table.

The hostess stood smiling. "I love your dress and it is so good to see a married couple going out on an evening. You are so lucky."

Todd spoke up. "Just good friends is all."

"Let me remind you sir you had better be changing that and soon. Ladies such as this come along very seldom in a lifetime."

The best he could do was blush a scarlet red. Nitto just smiled at him. She glanced down at the menu and her earring caught the light of a candle and her features jumped out at him. She had caught his attention for certain. It was at that very moment Todd knew his life was about to change. He had nothing to go back to Texas for except his children. He knew what he wanted. She looked up and smiled at him. "Everything ok Nanuq?

"Yes perfect Nitto. Just lost in thought and find it hard to take my eyes off of you is all."

"Anything you want to share with me?

"Not that I want to share just yet." He smiled. "A man has to keep some things to himself sometimes."

She again leaned forward and took his hand. "You have such a way with me Todd. I always feel so special."

"Just as long as you are around Sachs I want you to know I care for you dearly."

"The same goes for me. Nitto I will be staying around, no plans to leave this is the first place I have felt so much peace. One thing I need to do is learn the language."

"Like I said it is simple and an easy language to learn. You can practice on me as much as you like."

"One word comes to mind." He smiled and took her hand and held it. "Kuluk is one I have been feeling."

She looked at him and tilted her head off to one side. "You know what Kuluk means in our language Todd?

"Yes, love is what I have been feeling for you for a long while Nitto."

She smiled, "See how easy the language is Todd. I know the word well and I have felt the same about you since the day I watched you get off the plane when you arrived."

He smiled, leaned over and kissed her lightly on the lips. In that case I have already conquered the language barrier."

"You have a very good start Nanuq." She leaned close into him. You have done very well."

The waitress smiled and set the meal down. "Have to like a man who listens so well." No more was said.

The food was wonderful, far richer than he had become accustomed to eating this last several months. The small corner of the dining room had been set aside for dancing. The piano played softly in the corner and he took her into his arms and guided her across the floor. "It has been a long while since I held anyone this close. Thank you for coming here with me."

"Pleasure is all mine Todd. It is good to get away and see how the rest of the world lives." She looked up at him and smiled. "You are a great dancer."

They spent several minutes dancing and the heat of their bodies being so close to each other was obvious. It was Todd who finally said, "I think we had better sit down Nitto. You are a very beautiful lady and it is better we be a little further apart than we are right now." They finished dessert. He stopped and paid the bill and they headed in the direction of the ballroom the hotel had.

The show started at 8 pm sharp and it was even more than what they had been told it would be. The Vaudeville show had been perfected over the years with Can Can dancing and many comical skits. At one point during the show they had taken Nitto up on stage and two of the actors pretended to be swooning her. Nitto had played along very well. The crowd played along and before long Nitto had been proposed to by one of the actors. She leaned over and kissed him on the cheek and said. "See that big guy out there. Sorry to tell you he is my man."

The actor jumped up and said "I defy you who ever you are to come up here and take this lady away from me."

With the prodding of several people around him Todd stood and climbed the stairs. "I am here he said and the two actors raced to see who could hide behind the other. He bent and took Nitto's hand and said shall we my dear. I think I have made my point tonight?

Nitto would not be upstaged and leaned in closely. "Oh great Nanuq of the north, thank you for sparing me from these evil men."

He turned and started to walk off the stage, stopped and look down at her. "In that case if you are not willing to marry this man, would you marry me?

The crowd all laughed and he bent on one knee. "Nitto would you marry me, I have little but I would love to be your husband."

The crowd stopped laughing when they saw her tears appear. She stood for the longest time looking deeply at him. She slowly turned and smiled at the two actors. "Sorry fellows but it looks like I will be getting married to this man."

He stood and took her into his arms as the crowd erupted in applause. The two actors stepped out encouraged the crowd as he bent and kissed her. It was then the full impact of what he had said hit him. He had asked and she had said yes. They walked from the stage and back to their seats and the many along the way reached out and congratulated them.

The two actors watched on and finally they started to kibitz back and forth and before long one said. "Now that is one hard act to follow."

The rest of the show went past and it was like they had missed it all. Nitto curled in close and whispered in his ear "Yes of course yes Todd Morris. I have waited a long while for you to come, my prayers have been answered."

When the show was over they started to leave like everyone else. Many again congratulated them. They could only smile. Once away from the crowds Nitto pulled him into her arms and whispered, "Of course Todd Morris, Of course. You certainly know how to take a girl out on a date and sweep her off her feet. I so love you Nanuq."

They took a walk around the hotel. The night was cold but neither noticed. Todd remained quiet until she asked are you ok?

"Better than ok, do you realize Nitto that we are engaged to be married and you know nothing about me?

"What is there to know other than you are a kind, compassionate and very caring man who has so much love to offer. Small Wave loves you dearly. That is all that I need, nothing more."

The night ended with them standing in the hallway of the hotel and he kissed her softly on the lips. She responded by pulling herself in as closely as she could to him. They kissed for the longest while and this time it was Nitto that pulled back. "I think I better say good night Todd. See you in the morning. I love you and the heart you have."

Todd watched as she slipped into her room. He stepped back and turned and opened the door to his room. Just before the door closed he heard a soft voice "Good night Nanuq. Rest well and know that you are loved." It was followed by a faint click of the lock on her door.

That night he lay thinking of what had taken place. It would be yet another sleepless night as he dreamt of her and what the future would hold. They would be married soon. He would again have a family.

Chapter Twenty Three

"Flying Home"

Over breakfast the following morning they held hands and talked about what the future would mean to them and Small Wave. Where they would live and how that would effect them. The choice was an easy one. The trailer he had would never be suitable so it would be Nitto's house. She was excited and already planning a few changes to the small home. "We can make it work Todd. Do you know that once we are married you automatically qualify for your indefinite work visa and Treaty Status?

He smiled, "That was not what I had in mind Nitto?

She laughed, "I know but there are several things that come into play when you marry a native. You qualify for all sorts of benefits as well, tax breaks, health care and many other things. You will be treated the same as any of my people."

"Still not what I had in mind Nitto," He smiled and took her hand. "I was thinking more of the fact that we will be together all the time, you know the three of us."

Nitto blushed and looked at him. "Todd I do pray you will not be disappointed. This has all happened so very quickly?

"Nitto, never doubt that you are beautiful and very desirable and have a great deal to offer. We will be fine and I know that we will have the blessing of Small Wave and the community. Now we need to go shopping, he took her hand and they walked down main street until they found a small jewellery. "Lets get a ring on your finger and make this official."

An hour later Nitto stood looking at the ring on her hand. It is perfect Todd. I know you wanted more but I love this and the design is perfect. One small diamond is all that is needed. Thank you."

Todd had something else in mind but Nitto had insisted on simplicity and it was what she wanted. He was one not to argue. He only smiled watching the joy she had. "As long as you are sure Nitto?

"Positive, thank you Nanuq."

They packed up at the hotel and took a cab to the airport. An hour later after doing all his ground checks and securing the cargo, filed their flight plan, they had clearance to take off.

The day was clear as he applied full throttle and the plane started to take off. He sensed it was a little sluggish on take off but it seemed to clear itself and lifted off the south end of the runway. He made a long sweeping turn over the city of Whitehorse and they turned to the Northeast towards home. Nitto sat looking at her hand and the ring and smiled.

They had flown a few hours when again he heard the same sound that he heard at take off. The plane shuddered a few times There was no hiding his concern this time because Nitto had heard it as well.

"What is that Todd?

"Not sure, thinking it may be a fuel problem. He checked the gauges and said. "We have lots of fuel but I wonder if there may have been some water in the fuel in Whitehorse." The engines sputtered at the same time, again coughed and died completely. They were flying at the 9500 foot assigned level. He reached for the microphone and called in Whiskey-Whiskey-Alpha-Bravo 29 we have lost power, at 9500, mark location."

"Roger WWAB 29 we have your co-ordinates." He looked at Nitto who had turned far lighter in colour than normal.

He reached over his hand. "Nitto all will be fine, make sure your seat belt is done up well. We are going to have to land." He tipped the wings side to side and attempting to get some new fuel into the lines. It fired coughed and caught. They climbed 1000 feet and it sputtered again and died and all went quiet. He rocked the wings again and attempted to start the engine. It would only sputter and stop again.

"WWAB 29 we are going to have to put down. The only clearing I have is a large lake. I would say it may be Great Bear Lake the Northern end. I see a long beach I may be able to land on. Better call search and rescue and Sal in Sachs Harbour and give him our position. Starting our decent now." Nitto was busy making sure she was secure and helped him get into his seat belt while he fought the dead plane. The beach was shorter than he thought the closer they got. Todd made a long low approach only a few feet over the tree tops and at the very last minute adjusted to full flaps and pulled the plane into a steep stall to slow it. Then pushed the yoke fully forward, The wheels touched down and immediately cut ruts into the mucky sand. He feathered the nose up and the end of the sandy beach came fast. At the very last minute the nose dropped and both props cut into the muddy sand and crashed to the ground and they came to a stopped thrusting them both forward. His head slammed into the yoke and his world went black.

The next thing he heard was a rustling beside him. Nitto was moaning, an acidy smell filled the air. Shorted out wiring was the smell. He opened his eyes and the cabin was filled with a light haze of smoke. He willed himself awake and looked at Nitto. She was moving at least, are you ok?

She lifted her head and moaned again. Yes I think so. I have a great deal of pain in my right shoulder but I think I am fine. How about you?

"I think so, a bad bump on the head but all seems ok." His vision was clouded with a crimson mist and he could see her looking at him with horror in her eyes. He reached up and attempted to wipe his eyes and looked at his hand. It was bright red with blood. "We had better get out of here Nitto to safety and see what we can salvage.

"Here I better check that cut. It is very deep Todd."

"Later lets get what we can from the plane. First aid kit, emergency supplies and rifle. Take all your luggage. Best get it all away in case we have a fire started from the electrical damage." He again wiped the blood from his eyes and unsnapped her seat belt. My side door is buckled, check yours?

Nitto reached with her left hand and pulled the handle. The door popped open but was jammed as well. She put her shoulder to it and cried out in pain. "Looks to me you may have something more than just a sore shoulder happening. Here let me get turned around." He positioned himself and with one swift kick the door flew open and the cold draft filled the cabin. "You first Nitto, lean back into me and get your feet out. Try and hold your arm and shoulder steady. Just slide down the wing and I will be right out."

She cried out as she moved. Once out she slid down the wing and once her feet hit the ground she gave another cry. He slid out next to her and helped her get several yards away from the wreckage. The cold wind was coming off the water and he went to the emergency compartment and took out an extra large down filled sleeping bag and helped Nitto slide inside and he zipped her in. "I should be taking care of that nasty cut," she whispered.

"Later. Right now you stay put. I will get the rest of the stuff I can. I will be right here. You need to stay warm."

"Thanks for getting us safely on the ground Todd. I will go on a date with you anytime." Nitto closed her eyes. He checked her forehead and he could tell she was going into shock. He left and started to rummage through the plane to see what he could find for supplies. He carried it all out and covered it with a small tarp. The snow had started to come down and in the western skies the clouds had turned a deep blue/black. This was going to be a bad storm. He would need to build a shelter.

Todd found a large orange tarp, an axe and some wire and got started. Within an hour he had built a structure around Nitto. It resembled a tent open on one side. The closed side stopped the wind from blowing in. Nitto was still resting but was shivering from the cold and the shock she was in. He built a fire and climbed in beside her for a few minutes. "I will need to get some firewood for the night and get some water boiling. We have a few things to eat, some raisins, peanuts, two chocolate bars and some packaged soup. I found some fishing line and a hook and some snare wire. Sal was fairly well prepared." He touched her forehead again and it was cold and clammy. "Do you think you can sit up. I think we better check that shoulder of yours. I found some Aspirin. It is all we have for medication."

Nitto sat up grimacing at the pain and he helped her out of her winter parka and she started to open her blouse. She stopped long enough to smile. "I guess you will get to see more of me than I wanted," and she laughed. "Lets just say this is a sneak peek. I would say keep your eyes closed but afraid that would do no good. I really am a modest girl you know, but right now this is very different."

She slipped the blouse over her shoulder and it was obvious her shoulder had been dislocated. The bruises she had on her chest and shoulder showed she had slammed hard against the yoke on her side of the plane. "I think considering where we are, lets just say I had my eyes closed."

"You will need to reset this for me Todd. You will need to straighten my arm and give one hard pull. I have seen this done before. Be prepared because I will likely pass out with the pain."

"Oh I hate to bring you more pain Nitto. Can I just wrap and immobilize your arm instead?

"You could but this will need to be reset. Please go ahead. Better give me a few of those aspirin now. Leave this for a few minutes and then lets get this over with."

"Here," he said and gave her the aspirin. I will be back in a few minutes better get you covered again." He pulled the sleeping bag up over her shoulders. Now rest a while I will be right back."

Todd busied himself with getting more wood, got a fire started and checked the radio which was dead. He took a few bright red berries from a tree, attached one to the hook, next he tied a small rock to the end of the line. He tossed it out and let it settle to the bottom and tied the line to an overhead branch. He filled a small aluminium cooking pot with water and set it beside the fire. Nitto was resting. He twisted the snare wire into three snares and placed them on what he thought were rabbit or Ptarmigan runs. He made a large pile of wood into a signal fire with plenty of green boughs to generate lots of smoke. With plenty of dry material below. He cut several small spruce bows with an axe and stacked them all around to keep the kindling dry in case they had to light it fast if a search plane would be heard.

Next he cut a large pile of boughs for the inside of the shelter to insulate them from the cold ground. He carried them all over and again Nitto stirred in pain. "Sorry honey we are going to have to move you outside for a minute while I make the bed for us. This will keep us up off the ground. Then we will need to reset that shoulder. I have some soup ready for you. Better get something warm inside of you while you are awake." He helped her outside and covered her again while he spread a foot of boughs all over the inside. He poured two packages of soup mix into the boiling water and stirred it with a small stick. He helped her inside again and gave her a cup of steaming broth."

"It is time Todd, lets do this and get it over with. I am no good to you like this. I see that the wound on your forehead has finally stopped bleeding. That moss over there, the bright green moss will draw out any infection. Just hold it in place with your hand or tie something around your head to hold it there. Remember to have some soup as well. Promise me that you look after you as well."

"I promise he smiled and helped her lay down."

Sorry while you were away I had to take off my bra. It was cutting into my shoulder. Please do not think less of me."

"Quiet now Nitto. Lay back and let me do this for you. I reset a friends shoulder once on the football team' so you will need to trust me."

Nitto lowered the sleeping bag and blushed slightly. He took her arm into his hands and smiled and said "I love you." Before she could respond he gave a sharp pull and he heard a pop. Nitto just looked at him as she started to fall into a world of blackness. "So sorry sweetheart, better to not be waiting for it. Now you rest as he reached over and buttoned her blouse and slipped the parka over her shoulders and zipped up the sleeping bag. He rolled up

some of his clothes and made a pillow and slipped it under
her head.

Chapter Twenty Four

"Growing Storm"

Todd sat back and watched Nitto rest. The groaning
had stopped and all was quiet except for her steady
breathing. He stood and stepped outside and was
immediately met with a blistering wind from the West. It
was snowing hard now and the last rays of daylight were
upon them. He stood looking at the destruction that lay all
around him. Sals plane would become one of the relics of
the north. It was bent and twisted beyond repair. The
wing on the pilots side was half torn off with jagged pieces
of outer skin revealing a mass of tangled wires and cables.
He checked all over the plane and there were no signs of

fuel leaks. He again went through the entire plane in search of anything they could use. He did find a full box of ammunition for the rifle. It was only a 22 caliber but it was better than nothing. He searched through all the suitcases and found a pair of sheer black nylons that would hold the moss in place. He smiled thinking of Nitto wearing such a thing. "Give your head a shake Morris, look at where you are."

With his knife he cut out some of the moss and slipped it into the stocking and tied it around his head. Almost immediately he could feel the moss starting to draw. He must look some cute he laughed at himself.

He returned to the lean to and sat looking at Nitto who was still asleep. It was then that it hit him. He started to pray and thank God for sparing them both. He found himself praying aloud. When he had finished he heard a faint whisper "Amen."

Nitto had come around again. He reached for the Aspirin bottle and shook out a few more and gave her some cold water. "We are all set for the night Nitto, you get some rest and I will be here if you need me. Just call when you awake again."

"I will, my that is a pretty bandage, shame on you Todd for going through a ladies personal things. You do look good in my dainties, sorry they are not the place I wanted to have you see them. You are very creative I see." She smiled faintly. "My shoulder is feeling better. Thank you for your prayers and may He rest upon you this night."

He bent and kissed her lightly on the lips and she snuggled in close. "Are you going to be warm enough, I am sure we could both fit in here if you like?

"I will be fine, you rest and I will watch the fire. Hopefully you will feel better tomorrow then I may consider your offer. Just rest for now. Sorry there will be no coffee tomorrow."

"Yes there is I will teach you tomorrow, any plant that produces berries will make herbal tea with small amounts of natural caffeine. I have much to teach you as she lay her head back and closed her eyes again. I will make you an Inuit man Nanuq. You will be a great hunter and provide for many."

Todd lay in behind her looking outside, the wind was still howling. He again got up and hauled several long pieces of driftwood up from the shoreline. He lay them side by side so all he would have to do is push them into the fire to keep it going during the night. He wished he had Nanapi's mitts she had made. The old work gloves he had found were still better than nothing. The night was restless, he awoke to the increasing wind often. Each time checking Nitto and the fire. Once during the night he felt a hand on the side of his face and found Nitto smiling at him.

Morning brought even worse weather and they were completely socked in. He had gone out early and collected as many leaves as he could find off the berry branches. The ones that remained were still greenish brown. With a pocketful he returned and filled another old pot with water and set it to boil. His fishing line he had tossed out had frozen in the ice that had formed the night before. According to the reading of the thermometer that Sal had mounted on the windshield of the plane it was 22 below zero. He smashed the ice with a big log and started to pull in the line and could feel it had some weight. They had managed to catch a fair sized Arctic Char. He re-baited the hook and tossed it out again. This would feed them for a few days.

When he got back Nitto was sitting up and running a brush through her shiny black hair using her left hand. She smiled. "Is that Rose Hip Tea I smell? Look at you Nanuq of the north, you have brought some food home. I crashed with a good hunter at least."

He smiled and looked at her struggling to brush the right side of her hair. "Here allow me Nitto. You need to rest."

"But I must look terrible Todd."

He took the brush and with long strokes brushed her hair. "You will always be beautiful. There look at you Nitto."

Tears filled her eyes and rolled down her face. "Combing my hair is something that Small Wave has always loved doing. She would insist every night that she had to make my hair sparkle."

"Just like it is right now. Small Wave will again brush your hair Nitto. Just wait till this weather lifts and we will be found. Search and rescue will be grounded till it clears. They will find us as they know the area we are in."

"Maybe so Todd but these storms this time of the year have been known to last weeks on end. Nature has a mean side to her as well and always makes sure we know who the boss is. Last year we were closed in for nearly three weeks."

"According to our last location I would say that we are at the Northwest side of Great Bear Lake in the Northwest Territories. Sal has always said to stay with the plane. Norman Wells should be off in that direction a few hundred miles. Fort McPherson that way and Paulatuk that way. We are in a very isolated place but we have fish, tea and no doubt there is small game. We will be fine Nitto. Best of all we have God and each other, I will look after you. Small Wave is fine with Nanapi and Sal would have received word and everyone will be praying. For now we just need to focus on staying safe and warm."

He stuck his head outside and poured two cups of berry tea for them. It was strong and a little bitter but it warmed them. He gave Nitto a few more Aspirin and before long she was resting again. He lay beside her and looked at her and her beauty. He kissed her forehead and before long he was asleep beside her.

He awoke a few hours later and Nitto was putting wood on the fire. He was covered with the sleeping bag. She turned and smiled and passed him a piece of fish on a stick. "Eat Nanuq and then you rest, it is my turn to look after you."

"I have heard that two people can stay very warm when they are close together, especially when they are zipped into a sleeping bag, fairly common practice I have heard here."

"It is, first eat some fish and have more tea. Then we will see if that is the truth."

After they were finished Nitto slipped in beside him and he zipped the bag up. "You are right Nanuq, this legend of the North is a true legend. Now we rest."

"I have grown very fond of this legend." He drew her in close and the faint smell of shampoo filled his nose. "I do like this legend. What more a man ask for?

"For that matter what more could a lady ask for?

Chapter Twenty Five

"Long Nights-Short Days"

Todd carved another notch in the corner post of the lean to. This was the seventh day they would be spending and the weather had no signs of letting up. The mist and cloud cover hung low over the lake. The wind would slow some during the day and at night would again howl. The temperature this morning was -33 degrees below. Nitto was feeling much better and favoured her arm less each day. His wound had healed well. She took the nylon off and looked at the deep gash. "Better leave this off and allow the cut to dry a little today. It is looking much better."

"I think it all because of the choice of bandage material I found in your suitcase Nitto. It has nothing to do with the moss." He laughed and she slapped his shoulder then bent in pain.

"A good lesson for you. You should never strike the man who you have been sleeping with for the past 6 days. I think that is another legend I have heard from the North. Those who sleep together are to behave?

"Todd I need to tell you something." She hung her head then looked into his eyes. "Thank you for respecting my wishes and not trying to force me into something I would regret later. You are a very desirable man and there have been moments when you have kissed me that it would be so easy to let go and make love to you." She blushed again. "But you have never taken advantage of how vulnerable I find myself."

"Nitto, that is something I want us to save until we are married and not out here in this place like we are. It is something I want to be beautiful and filled with pleasure and joy. Not like this."

"Thank you," and she leaned over and kissed him lightly on the lips. "Right from the first time I laid eyes on you I knew you were the man God had intended for me. Something about you Nanuq that is so different than so many men. You are kind and gentle and have a special spirit that travels with you. What is it that makes a man like you?

He took her hands in his. "I have never told you very much about my life prior to coming to Sachs Harbour. I have not said much for fear of losing you. Time I shared this with you. Painful story but you should know."

She sat and smiled at him. "Over another cup of tea then Nanuq. I collected some leaves this morning. I do want to learn all about you. Then if you like I will tell you all about my life and how Small Wave came into being and such an important part of who I have become."

Over tea he started to tell his story of his marriage and his two children. He told her of the success of his business, his home and friendships with many. Then he explained what he found out about Marie his wife and Al Starsnick having an affair and what he had done. Tears filled his eyes as the shame of it all took hold. "Those were the hardest few years I spent in life. The loss of the business and my family. The time I spent in prison took all the anger and bitterness from me. It was there that I again come to Christ and begged His forgiveness for what I had done. It was there that He started to change me from a very angry bitter man to what you are seeing today."

"And all these people that signed you the card Todd, who are they."

"People at a Mission, a soup kitchen. I had nothing and nowhere to go. I was sleeping in back alleys and scrounging for what ever I could find. I was fighting off the addiction I had for Cocaine. The Mission was a place where I was welcomed and accepted without the need of telling my story. They simply loved, a model that should be adapted the whole world over." He paused and looked off at the fire. "Nitto it is the model I see taking place here in the North where people depend on each other and share in all they have." He wiped the tears from his eyes. "It is just simply the way. I still recall the day I landed and a Native man from far away shared his Caribou with everyone. He passed me a piece of meat covered in blood.

There I stood about as far North as a man could be and a total stranger shared his wealth with me without question of who I was or anything. That Nitto is the way of love that God calls us all to live by."

"It is who we are Nanuq, who you have become. You are now one of us. You see you give from here and she touched his chest. It is called Naglingniq. It is much the same as Kulak.(Love) It is what I feel for you. It comes from here and she touched her chest."

"I truly hope that does not mean pity."

She laughed and took his face in her hands. "Nanuq my big Polar Bear. The word Naglingniq means love from the heart in the purest of sense. It is all I feel for you. What happened in the past is in the past. You see the way my people think is what ever has happened has happened. What is to come will come. What we do today in the form of kindness is what is really important. The more Naglingniq we give today the more that will come back to us. That man that gave you some of his meat Nanuq gave from here, the heart. He did not give from a sense of duty or as a form of payment. It came from his heart and you receiving it with a smile is all that counted."

"It was just a complete shock to me because it is certainly not the way in the South."

"No matter you accepted it and he was honoured you did. Being a white accepted here in the north is an honour and you have been accepted in the community. Many have spoken of you and that steadfast presence you have about you. What sealed your position was the successful hunt you were on and bringing much needed food to the community."

"Speaking of providing. I had better collect some wood before nightfall and check the snares, maybe we have something that will give us some meat tonight."

"Good and I will help. There are many Arvinggag here. I have seen many tracks. I will see if I can catch some. They are good roasted and have been a staple for my people for years."

He looked at her with a questioning look.

"Arvinggag are lemmings. They are of the mouse family but have more nutritional value. Trust me they are good Nanuq. Now that you are Inuit you will need to learn the language."

"Mouse family, really now and you eat them. Well we will see." He laughed. "By the look of the weather I think we have time. Even though we are stranded Nitto, I would not want to be stranded with anyone else but you." His smile brought on hers and they went about preparing for the long night ahead.

Chapter Twenty Six

"Closing Weather"

The following morning it would be hard to find anything a few feet away. It was like they had been wrapped in a cocoon of mist and snow. They had collected enough wood and there had been two Arctic Hares caught in the snares the night before.

"Okalik" Nitto sounded out the word slowly and pointed at the two rabbits.

"Okalik" he laughed and pointed. "Rabbit," and held them in the air and shook them. "Okalik, Nanuq caught Okalik for his Naglingniq."

"Very good Nanuq, Nanuq caught rabbits for his love. I am very impressed."

He beat on his chest and she laughed.

Nitto reached for the pot and scooped up some clean snow and melted it and added some leaves. I will make tea. Glad we have lots of wood and food. This is a day to stay close to the shelter. We could get lost quickly in this weather."

He smiled and pointed at the sleeping bag. "It is what they made these for. Have I mentioned that I really like sleeping with you Nitto. Not that sure I will be able to ever sleep alone again after the many days here."

"Traditional courtships with my people are generally short. The head of the household which would be Nanapi would determine if you are suitable for me. Once you have been approved the ceremony follows quickly." She blushed again. "Nanapi has already approved by giving you some of her mitts. You will still need to go through the formality of asking her in person. Be prepared as she may take a few weeks to think about it."

"Not sure if I can wait that long."

"You have no choice in the matter. Our people do not agree with people living together. The Inuit are changing slowly in the south but up here in the North the morals and values are still held in high esteem. I have heard stories of young men and ladies who have broken tradition and they have been shunned and forced from communities."

"That is far to serious a fate Nitto. I will be asking Nanapi as soon as we get back. Here let me get the tea, then I want to hear all about you."

He poured two cups of steaming tea and passed her one. "Thank you, you are a good provider. I just want you to know that your past has not changed the way I think of you. I pray that you accept that coming from my heart."

"I do and Nitto no matter what you say I promise to not judge."

"I was a restless child from the time I can remember. I have no idea what started it but I always felt there was more than what Sachs Harbour offered. A family of whites came in from the south to run the cannery." She slipped into the sleeping bag and motioned for him to join her. "They had a daughter Jennie who was about 16 and I was twelve. She had been around you might say. She shared stories of the men and the boys she had slept with. She taught me about the birds and the bees in some ways. Well at least explained how it all worked."

"I was so embarrassed, I recall that much. It has always been the northern way to go to your parents with questions." She looked into her tea cup and set it aside. "I simply came out one night at supper and asked my parents about sex. Dad asked what I knew and when I told him he beat me to within an inch of my life. They both assumed I had experience." Tears filled her eyes. "Two weeks later both Mom and Dad were lost at sea in a freak wind storm that carried them away from the hunting party. They were never found or heard from again. I had never been able to make peace with them. It still breaks my heart to think of them not knowing that I was still pure and what I spoke of was from Jennie. Later I learned that

Nanapi had slapped my father across the face for even thinking such a thing of me."

"I have a feeling Nitto, that if they had survived they would have been asking your forgiveness."

"I like to think that at least. There was a young man in the village that I had great feelings for. His name was Netlic. He was from the south and came every year to hunt and help. Nanapi could see that we were attracted and thought it best I be sent away to be trained in something in the South. She had found an ad from an Inuit newspaper, the Government was offering free schooling and I was sent to Vancouver, British Columbia to the University. Now I think she did it to protect me from Netlic. He was very demanding and very much aware. I was so young and naive, Nanapi was just protecting me." She searched his eyes and carried on.

"One complete floor of the dorms had been set aside for the Native population. One wing was boys and the other was girls."

"I had been attending classes for about two months and one day I ran into Netlic. He was taking a course and we started to see each other again. He spoke badly of Nanapi and yet I agreed to see him. He had changed, he became more demanding. He had found alcohol and drugs and he slowly started to lose his heritage. I stopped seeing him and he was very angry. Late one night while I was walking back to dorms he attacked me from behind and forced me into the trees and raped me." Again the tears formed in her eyes.

"His breath was horrible and the pain I suffered was terrible. He was so forceful he caused considerable damage. I needed surgery as a result. Nothing could stop the rumours on Campus. I was blamed and asked to leave. The only place I could come back to was Sachs Harbour. The day I was leaving I learned that Netlic had committed suicide and was found hanging from a light fixture in his room. The note he left was simple. "I have brought shame to Nitto and to my people. It is for this I do what I have chosen to do. Judge not Nitto."

"I am so sorry Nitto, what a horrible thing to have happen. Rape is such a violation of the human heart."

She cried for a little while then started to speak again. "I came back to Sachs Harbour and lived with Nanapi. It was then I missed my first period and then the second. By this time the community had learned of what had happened to Netlic and the questions started. I told Nanapi of what had taken place and that I had missed my period and thought I may be pregnant. It was confirmed at the doctors office in Yellowknife."

"We returned and again it is uncommon for a single girl to be pregnant because of the beliefs and all. I was judged and some shunned me. At one of the feasts Nanapi stood and her voice was heard. She spoke of the love we were to have for each other. She spoke of the child I was carrying as a gift from God even though it had been conceived in rape. I recall that night that she stood and slapped the table with her walking stick and the entire assembly sat in shock."

"Her words were few but they were heard. If anyone of you dare judge this innocent girl, this is what you shall get from me." Nitto laughed. "She held that staff high in the air and waved it back and forth and again struck the table. She took my hand and we walked home and the very next day there were boxes of food and baby gifts all over the front step. That was my Nanapi and she has stood by me all these years."

"Now there is a wonderful story. Know that you are not judged. Now what say we just spend the day cuddled in close and pray that the weather lifts so we can get back to our family at Sachs Harbour. From here in in Nitto it is me that they will have to answer too should they judge you or Small Wave or for that matter Nanapi. We will be fine Nitto. We will be just fine."

"I know Nanuq, I know, never been a doubt in my mind. God as been with us the entire time. Now rest."

Chapter Twenty Seven

"Sky Lifting"

He counted 23 days while he carved the notch in the corner post. She smiled.

"That is some date you take your girls on Nanuq. Hope they are not all this adventuresome. If they are well count me in. You have done a great job of looking after me. It looks like the weather is clearing finally. You know something funny Todd. I have not been one bit worried the whole time I have been here with you."

"Nor I with you being here with me. I would hate to crash land again but if I ever do I hope it is with you. This adds a new dimension to the term I have fallen for you. Literally falling from the sky. I had better get the signal fire checked and ready should we hear a plane. They will likely be out looking for us today."

"Then that calls for a celebration. Look what I have," and she lifted the pail that had once held parts for the DC-3. Inside were five Lemmings.

He turned his nose up. "Really I think we could do better than rodents to eat."

"Now look Mr Nanuq. I have eaten what you have put before me this past three weeks. Let me cook you a fine delicacy from my people. Get used to it because it is part of some cuisine you will not find anywhere."

"Yes ma'am. I will attend to the mans work while you dispatch of those hairy little things. I guess once will be fine." He kissed her on the forehead and left to attend to his signal fire. He added more material and shook the snow off the bows. He brushed the snow off the bright red wings of the aircraft and lay out as many bright objects as he could on the now solid ice in a pattern of SOS.

"The finest meal in the North is ready great white hunter. Come and face your worst fear. I promise it will not hurt."

He sat by the fire and she passed him one of the small rodents that had been roasted on a stick. He watched as she bit into one and made a sound of joy. "Now you big guy. Come on they are dead and won't bite."

He reluctantly went to open his mouth and just then he heard the sound of a far off aircraft. He jumped up and took a handful of burning sticks and ran and lit the signal fire. It caught right away and he added some green bows and immediately the white smoke rose high in the air. The sound of the aircraft grew faint then he could here it sharply bank and come back. The sound was distinctive it was a helicopter and it grew louder and louder. They both stood and waved their arms in the air. It made a wide circle. The bright yellow and red colours were those of search and rescue. It slowly descended and landed a few yards down the beach and the door opened.

"Word has it you folks may be looking for a ride. Looks like this one is here to stay for awhile. Captain James Brown is the name. He walked over and stuck out his hand. "At your service. That was some landing young man. Care to teach that one to some of my boys."

"No sir, good to see you folks."

"Are you ok. Come aboard. I have someone wanting to see you. Better bring along anything you want to bring along."

"Do you have room for some aircraft parts. It was my freight until I landed here at least. Kind of important. Parts are for an old DC 3 that is in Sachs."

"I know I have been hearing all about that old girl." Just then Todd looked and there was Sal climbing out of the helicopter and limping with one crutch over to him.

Tears fell from his cheeks. "If you had any idea of how much I have been praying for you two and look at you both in good condition. He stepped and and gave Todd a big hug. Well done son, very well done."

Todd pointed at the wreckage. "Who cares about that, what is important is that you are both alive. Nitto you are such a sight for these old eyes. Any chance an old timer can get a hug."

"Of course Sal, you can always have one of those from me."

"Lets see what we have here for freight, some guys have all the luck getting hugs and all."

"Captain is there a chance a girl could get a hug?

"Well lets see, I have never seen anything against it in the manual. Come here girl and if it is there what the heck we can break the rules." Nitto reached in and gave him a kiss on the cheek and whispered, "Thank You."

20 minutes later they had all the parts on board. The fires out and were about ready to take off when Todd called out. "One other thing I forgot, sorry gents but some things you never leave behind." He unbuckled himself and slid the door open and ran to the lean to. He came running back with the sleeping bag rolled up. "Just a little something I hate to leave behind."

Nitto just smiled and blushed.

The flight back to Sachs Harbour was warm and cozy as they related all that had taken place since they crashed. Sal sat and smiled. "The one thing you did that was right son was you stayed with the plane. We tried to come out but this front came in and we have been grounded the entire time. The Captain and his co-pilot Benny here have been held up at your place the entire time. They landed the day we got the call and well the rest has been a waiting game. You two ok. I see that you have a good bump on the head. What about you Nitto?

"Nothing really, just a dislocated shoulder that Nanuq here reset. Other than that as snug as a bug in a rug, thanks to this old sleeping bag you had on board. Mighty comfortable for two."

Sal was quiet for a few minutes then leaned over and gave Todd a stare. "I hope you behaved yourself young man?

Todd started to say something then Nitto raised a hand. "Sal you have nothing to worry about. Todd was a perfect gentleman. God had His eye on us the whole time."

"Good thing or I would beat you with my stick here. Darned good thing."

"Sal I have a favour to ask of you?

"Well what is it Todd, come on spit it out man. In the North we never mince words. Just say what is on your mind. If you are concerned about your job, you still have one."

"No not that and he slipped off the glove on Nitto's left hand. I was wondering if you would be my best man at the wedding is all?

Sal sat for a long while and then smiled. "It would be an honour and indeed a privilege as long as I do not have to wear a tie. Congratulations you two. Why in blazes do you think I sent you south together anyway, just for some parts? He laughed and looked up and smiled. "Thank You Father for answered prayer. Yes Sir thank You."

They made a circle over Sachs and and slowly touched down as the first of the people arrived. Before the rotors had stopped they were crowding in. The doors swung open and Nanapi was waiting. Once she spotted Nitto and Todd she looked to the heavens and raised her hands.

It was then that Small Wave ran forward and hugged her mom. The entire time chattering away in Inuit and pointed to the heavens."

Todd climbed from the helicopter and Small Wave came running and threw herself into his arms. The crowd gave a roar and watched the little girl kiss him all over his face. Yes they were home indeed. Many came forward and patted him on the back and spoke to Nitto.

Todd turned and looked at the Captain and said "Thank You."

"Is it any wonder we do what we do my friend. I see you have family here. Go be with them and thank you for what you did back there. The proof of a good pilot is how he reacts under adverse conditions. You have passed the test. Welcome to the North Todd Morris. Much as I hate to say this. Hope to never see you again." He turned and waved at his co-pilot and he started the chopper. The people backed away and they lifted off.

As fast as they came the people had left, leaving only himself, Nitto and Small Wave. "Mind if I walk you home Nitto. It has been a long date but I think it only proper I get you back home ok."

I should hope so Nanuq. You will come for breakfast in the morning I hope. I have a special surprise for you. Lets say when ever you get there."

"I would not miss it. The order of the day for the lady is a nice warm bubble bath. Lots of bubbles and please stay in there and enjoy yourself."

"I will, of course it will be better when I can share it with someone special." She blushed.

"It will be indeed. After all I have been sleeping with you for how long. Time I make a decent woman out of you I would say."

"I should think so."

Small Wave just chattered the whole time walking back. It was good to be home.

Chapter Twenty Eight

"Her Approval"

After Todd had delivered Nitto and Small Wave back to their home he slowly walked along the beach again and prayed and thank God for His hand of protection upon them over the past several days. They like the many before would become the legends of the past who had lived through such and ordeal. He stopped and sat on a rock and looked out over the ocean thinking of the final moments that Nitto's parents must have faced. He wondered if there had been any remorse on the part of her father over doing what he had to Nitto.

He thought about his son Jeff and daughter Linsey. He wondered where they were and what had become of them. He prayed they had been told of the better times by Marie. His prayer was it had not all been bad. He had taken little time with them as children as the business had taken all his time. He sat and looked at the ocean and prayed for them no matter where they were. He determined if he were to ever leave here he would find them.

After a long hot shower Todd Morris lay down in his bed that night knowing what had taken place over the past 23 days would change his life forever. He again stood and read the card of all the people at the Mission and the staff at the rehab centre. Yes they had done well. He lay with the card in his hand and prayed for all of them and prayed that God would touch them all for what they had done for him.

He awoke around seven to that infernal clock making its noise. As much as he hated it before all of a sudden it sounded much better. He drew a very hot bath and even added some dish soap to give some bubbles. He lay back and enjoyed the feel of the water listening to the small bubbles popping all around him. It was close to 9 when he knocked on Nitto's door.

Small Wave opened the door and with one leap was in his arms. She placed her hand on the side of his face and whispered Nakumi Nanuq. (Thank You)

"Ilaaki, Small Wave." (You are Welcome)

He took off his boots and parka and stepped into the small kitchen and there sat Nitto and Nanapi. They were holding hands and Nanapi stood and in very broken english she spoke. "Thank you Todd, you safe with Nitto."

"You are welcome Nanapi."

She led him over to Nitto and took her hand and placed it in his. She smiled and nodded and spoke one word. "Yes."

He looked at Nitto and Nanapi and smiled. Small Wave wanted up again and he lifted her. She smiled and said the word, "Yes."

Nanapi took both their hands and in a short prayer in her native tongue she prayed for them holding their hands together. Then stopped and looked at Todd and spoke again in a long sentence. The best he could do was smile. Then Nitto translated.

"Nanapi is known among our people for her words of wisdom. Generally what she speaks into people comes true. In the white Christian world these people are known as having the gift of being prophetic." She smiled and Nanapi spoke again. This time her hands started to shake. When she was done she turned to Nitto and waited for her to speak.

"Nanapi tells of a man as big in heart as a bear who comes and provides for many. She tells of the man with the big heart owning flying birds that will take people and cargo to many places." Nitto hesitated and blushed. "She speaks of many babies who will be offspring Nitto and Nanuq."

When she had finished Nanapi again spoke and reached up and touched his face. Tears filled her eyes.

Nitto again spoke. "This same man known as Nanuq will bring much joy to a heart that was broken years ago through the loss of her parents and the father of Small Wave."

Again a silence fell over the room. Nanapi stood silent for several minutes then spoke again. This time she spoke softly. "Nanuq will find what is deep in his heart. She sees two young children, a boy and a girl who are white and living in a big city. All the pain will be gone and Nanuq's heart will be healed."

It was his turn to weep as he drew the older lady in and she held him tightly. She then stood back and spoke again.

Nitto translated again. "Nanuq's heart will be filled with joy over giving of himself. He will be even greater blessed with the many blessings he will receive in return. Nanuq and his new family will be filled with many years of good fortune and much love and food. So much they will share with many."

He took the older ladies hands and whispered the word Ilaaki (Thank You) and bowed slightly and kissed her forehead.

Then came much joy as Small Wave heard the words and kissed his cheeks. Nitto's stood and slipped into his other arm. "There it is done Todd, you have been approved to be married. All we need to do is see the Pastor here and we can be married anytime."

"Good in that case lets do it today after Church. We can speak to him then."

"Very well, better hurry and eat your special breakfast." She sat him down and brought out three Lemmings from the oven and set the plate before him. He looked in complete doubt at them.

"I could not just leave them. After all God provided them. I have added some spices. Try them and I bet you will like them."

He picked one up again and today there was no rescue helicopter to save him and he bit into the small carcass. The meat was tender and spiced right. It tasted different. It had a flavour that resembled rabbit but had a texture of pork. He smiled and cleaned the rest of the plate and sat back and smiled. "Well not all that bad once you get past they are rodents."

"Now I better get ready for Church Nanuq. I will leave all of you to sort through the language barrier. Maybe that will create a deeper desire for you to learn it."

Nitto came back into the room a few minutes later wearing a simple dress, slipped into her coat and smiled. "Come along all of you or we will be late."

The small church was filled to capacity. The pastor stood at the front of the church and led the congregation in singing in their native tongue. Even though some of the notes sounded familiar Todd was lost the better part of the service. He would need to learn this language.

After the people had left they found the Pastor standing at the back of the Church. "Pastor Robert it is a pleasure to meet a man with such a grasp for this language. Maybe I should be taking lessons from you?

"Be like me son and pay attention. Nitto here will teach you. I heard via the grape vine this morning we have a marriage coming up soon." He turned to Nitto. "What a blessing it is to hear. Small Wave will have a real father after all."

"When would be a good day to have the wedding. We can work around your schedule. I know that you need to come from Yellowknife?

"I do, I will be missing next Sunday as I have a family gathering. I will be back in two weeks. That would place the date the same as a regular service. I think it would be a great celebration."

"It would, that way we could have everyone here. What do you think Todd?

"Great plan."

"I mean not to be rude but I think you both have the wisdom of your years and premarital counselling is something we can forego. Would you be in agreement to simply get married. Otherwise I would need to spend sometime with you?

"We will be fine Pastor Robert, just be here. Matter of fact I will likely be the one that flies you back here."

Very well in that case we can talk man to man on the way over. Give me a chance to see where you are in your faith. Congratulations folks. Now I better get ready to leave. Sal is flying me back in a few minutes. The life of a travelling Pastor is a hard life."

Chapter Twenty Nine

"Traditions"

The following Thursday morning he was awakened at 4 am by a loud pounding on his door. He stood pulled on his pants and there stood three natives all dressed in warm clothing. One held up a harpoon and made a motion towards the ocean and grunted.

It was obvious they wanted him to come along. He dressed in the warmest clothes he could find and followed them to their boats. "Oomiak's" is what they were called. Traditionally made with wood frames and covered in skins. The leader's name was Touwanny, a well respected hunter and leader of the men. He smiled at Todd and with his two hands he placed on either side of his nose he extended his fingers downward and grunted. Todd assumed it was some sort of tusked animal they were hunting for.

He had been passed a paddle and they pushed off and headed toward the outcropping of Arctic Island a mile to the Northwest. The Oomiak glided across the water. The air was cold but Todd was dressed warm. His hands were covered in Nanapi's mitts she had made. The hunter he was paddling beside motioned to the mitts and smiled. He spoke one word, "Good."

Todd nodded and smiled. He had no idea what he was getting into here. His borrowed rifle a .270 Browning Semi Automatic beside him. He would fine out soon enough.

They rounded the end of the first rocks and the leader raised a hand and all paddling stopped. He raised a rifle with a scope on it and scanned the rocks slowly left to right. He swung his hand slowly back making a paddling motion and they moved in towards the next set of rocks. He again raised the rifle and ducked low. He looked at Todd and made the motion that he should be ready with his rifle.

They slowly moved in and Todd was able to make out a large Walrus laying on the top of the rocks. The only sound was the surf gently lapping at the rocks. The grey colour was hard to distinguish but it looked like about thirty or better mammals had settled in. Many were just laying quiet. He could tell the men had done this before. He looked at them, all bent over low but still paddled slowly towards the rocks. They were about 100 yards away when the leader pointed at him and made a motion that looked big and ferocious and again placing his two fingers to what appeared as tusks downward. Todd assumed he was to take the largest mammal. They turned the boat sideways and each man raised his gun. The leader nodded at Todd and they waited for him to shoot first.

The large male with long tusks lifted his head and Todd took careful aim and squeezed off his first shot. The silence was broken with several shots that followed. He took aim at another and it too fell and he managed a third shot and the water turned red as the mammal hit its surface. Out of the twelve shots that were fired 9 animals were pulled from the rocks and the water. Each man smiled at Todd when they hauled his big bull into the boat. "Good Nanuq, Good." The leader spoke and slapped him on the back. "Nuliaq" (Good) He looked pleased as he ran his hand along the tusks.

They arrived back at the main town shortly after 9 in the morning and were met by many. They unloaded the days hunt and within minutes the leader gave the two tusks to Todd and motioned towards Nitto and again grunted. He had no idea what he was to do. The work stopped. Nitto finally spoke. "You are to give them to me as a showing you are a worthy hunter."

He moved slowly towards her and held out the two tusks. Each was about two feet long. She looked at them, then at him. Everyone seemed quiet until she smiled in approval.

Then the men all came around and patted him on the back. The leader stepped in front of him and pointed at his eye, then the rifle, then the tusks, then at Nitto. "Good, happy." He slapped Todd on the back. Good." He said again.

The day was a busy one. They cut up all the meat and it was spread throughout the community. The men would occasionally cut off a piece of fat and eat it. The leader of the hunting party kept trying to have Todd eat some. Finally he tried a small piece and they all laughed at him and the face he made. The leader rubbed his tummy and smiled. "Good," He said.

After they were all done Nitto smiled and said "Come for supper tonight. We are having a traditional pre wedding supper as a couple who are to be married. Later we will join in a dance of celebration to the Creator for what he has given."

"I will be there even if I need to eat Lemming to show these people that I love you."

"Good and then after we are married you need to carve me something with these tusks to show your love for me.

It is something you have to do on your own. I cannot help. This is one thing you must do with your skills as a hunter. All I am suppose to do is accept them and place them in a prominent place in the home. See you at 6, you did well today Nanuq."

Nothing had gone to waste that day. He watched as the remaining three men packed up their guns and knives. Each stopped and smiled as they headed towards their homes. The leader stopped and spoke a few words and pointed at the rifle and then at Todd. "Good," was all he said as he headed off in the direction of his home. He stopped once more, turned and smiled and said Good Nanuq, Good."

The following morning Sal called him into the office. "The Department of transport needs a full report of the crash. They are about to launch and investigation. Nothing to be worried about, they are just trying to tie up some loose ends. I was told there was another aircraft that day that had the same issue but had managed to land safely. Just a formality. They tested the fuel in the other plane and found it to have water in the fuel. Happens in this weather. We are quiet today anyway. Lets get this out of the way. We have a wedding to plan you know."

Todd spent the better part of the day filling out all the paperwork for the government. They wanted it in his exact words what happened the day they crashed. Then came all the insurance papers. "Silly really I did not even know I was covered on that old girl. Who knows maybe enough of a claim coming back you and I can fly down to some auction in the south and find us another."

"Happy to do this Sal. Just sorry I lost your baby for you."

"That will be the last I hear of it. Just one of those horrid things that happens in this business. All I care about is that you two made it out ok. Be a lot harder off if I knew one or both of you had been lost. Just fill out the papers and never mind any about the loss of some plane. You should know that is all that counts anyway. Time to move on son, time to move on. Oh by the way the DC 3 should be up and running soon. Now there should be a blessing. Yes sir be great to have her back again."

Chapter Thirty

"Preparations"

Today would be the maiden flight of the newly repaired DC-3. He had pulled it out of the hanger and she sat on the runway with both engines running. The temperature had started to warm again and the snow had started to melt and small streams were washing down into the ocean. He stepped inside the hanger and pounded the slush off his boots, sound carried throughout its expanse.

He stepped into the small office and Sal was just finishing up some paperwork. "What say we get this old girl off the ground and see what she can do. Just let me get my gear on and we will be off to the races. We have a full load today. They have been holding some of the non essential freight for us so we will be heavy today." Sal reached around the corner in the small room and slowly got dressed in his gear. Todd noticed he was moving a little slower than normal.

"Are you feeling ok Sal?

"Not sure might have me a flu bug or something, been feeling a little off the last few days."

"What say we take sometime while we are in Yellowknife and see a doctor?

"I will be fine, I will lay up a few days after we get this freight here and you can take it from there getting it out and about. Ok Todd I think we have everything. Lets have this old girl slice some air again and make sure she is ready to fly."

With Sal at the controls and having filed their flight plan they had clearance to take off. Sal moved the throttles forward and the old DC 3 started to lumber down the runway. "Pressures are all looking good and all ok," Todd spoke into the headset.

"In that case lets see if she can fly." Sal pulled back on the yoke and the old plane went from the rough runway and into the air. Todd looked back and a vapour trail came off the wings from the humidity and the cooler air aloft. He again turned to the gauges and watched and all looked ok. He glanced over at Sal who was all smiles.

"All is checking out my friend. Looks like we are on our way to Yellowknife. I will make a long loop of 15 miles or so just to stay close to the runway. Then we can be away if all is holding." He again called the tower in Yellowknife and told them they were flying a circuit. All checked out and they banked to their heading and were on their way.

"Take over, I made us some coffee, care for a cup?

"Certainly, while we were grounded I missed out on your coffee Sal. You make it just the way I like it, strong and black. Those berry leaves cannot hold a candle to real coffee."

"By the look of the camp you made I would say you have done it before. Everything close at hand, certainly glad to know that you can look after things. The man that loses his head in situations like those is the one they find later frozen."

"True but all the courses they teach on survival in Texas are no match for the North country. I have been thinking about the whole thing and what it comes down too is nothing but good old common sense. Nitto was a great help to keep me focused."

"She is a beautiful lady. Her mother was a real looker. Those high cheek bones and the deepest blue eyes you have ever seen. Nitto's dad was a piece of work that one. Personally I think close to flipping out most of the time. Jealous of his wife something fierce."

"I recall once I was standing at a gathering talking to her. Just regular stuff you know and he came out of nowhere and shoved me aside and took her by the arm and dragged her away. The rest of the night she sat on her chair and he glared at me the whole evening. A mean streak in him that one. Here have a coffee."

"Thanks Sal. Nitto tells me they were lost at sea?

"They were. Nitto's dad had developed a bad cough. One day while he was out hunting I was asked to go to the house and fix the oil heater. Nitto's mom told me he was coughing up blood. Tuberculoses is what I suspect. When it gets to that point it is almost a death wish. Her mom shared with me she was afraid for her life because he was talking crazy. You know about ending it all and such. She had said that Nitto's dad had said that no other man would ever have his wife."

Sal looked out the window and he could tell it had bothered him. "So what you are saying is maybe it was not an accident?

"To the best of my knowledge she never told anyone else of her concerns. It was late in the year when it happened. The hunting party had left on a cloudy day. The winds had started to blow in from the Northwest. There had been a party of four boats, several men and only one woman, Nitto's mom. It was unusual for a woman to go on hunting trips, but he had insisted they have a helper along to cut the meat.

"They had been gone two days, a storm started brewing and they were due back. It was late evening when the hunting party arrived back. They were short one boat and two people."

"The men were very quiet, there was no hope of anyone going out and searching. The storm lasted three days before it cleared. I flew for days in hopes of finding something. There was nothing. No remains of any kind."

"Milatou the leader shared with me several days later of the concern he had. He said that Nitto's dad was one of the best hunters he had ever seen and never took chances."

"Milatou said it was common practice to tie all the boats together bow to stern for safety in high winds. That day Nitto's dad had waved it off and insisted on taking up the rear."

"Milatou just stood shaking his head when I asked him what had happened. He said all was fine then a few minutes later he turned and all he could see was Nitto's mom reaching out and her dad paddling away. That was the last anyone ever seen of them. Personally I think he decided to end it all and take her with him."

"That is so sad Sal."

"It is but in the end Nitto went to live with Nanapi. She was allowed to grow into a beautiful young lady."

"She has indeed, Nitto shared with me her life and some of the struggles and all. She speaks highly of Nanapi and her teachings."

"Nanapi and I have been good friends for many years. She went so far as to tell me once that I should have been the one to marry Nitto's mom should he have died. We do have a close connection Nanapi and I. The best of friends and I would trust that old girl with my life. That is one wise lady and she has a great gift of speaking into peoples life."

"I know, she spoke into mine."

"Looks like we are going to be landing soon. Good chatting with you. Proud of you and what you are doing with Nitto and Small Wave. Just be sure and look after them my friend."

Sal called into the tower at Yellowknife and they got clearance to land. "I can take over if you like. Better finish your coffee."

Sal took over and banked to the left and made a sharp turn. He could feel the G forces pushing him into the seat. "God I love that sound and the feeling of power. Nothing like these old birds man, nothing like them." They came in hot and fast and touched down and Sal applied the brakes. "Love to show these young pups at the airport what flying is all about." He laughed and pulled in front of the freight terminal and shut things down. "I would say she is up to snuff again and ready for some real work."

Four hours later they lifted off and the true nature of the plane showed her colours as she climbed slowly. "All yours my friend. I think I will take a little nap. Wake me before we land."

Shortly after he could hear the sound of Sal snoring loudly. He was glad that Sal had taken a chance on him and allowed him to come North. He would take this life over and above anything that was left in Texas.

Chapter Thirty One

"The Big Day"

He had taken the flight over to Yellowknife that morning and picked up Pastor Robert. They had talked at length of his life and his faith. Before they landed Robert had smiled at him. "You know brother you have had a difficult life and yet I sense this great peace about you. Nitto and Small Wave will be fine in your care."

"Thanks and I will be sure and look after them, just as God has called me to do."

"Come along then my friend, we have a wedding to attend. This is a great day."

The music played in the background. "Mesima was a Church Elder who had taught herself to play the old piano which was far out of tune. Occasionally she would hit a bad note and laugh and keep playing. Her heart was in the right place. He just smiled at her and she took the time to wave at him and missed several notes again.

Pastor Robert stood smiling and Sal stood beside him. Todd looked nervous. He had managed to find the best of his clothes, Nanapi had made him a vest of Caribou hide and it was hand beaded with all the native wild flowers. On the back in bright red letters was his name "Nanuq." She had been fussing over it for the past few weeks. She had also made him a pair of traditional mukluks. They were also hand beaded and lined with Fox fur. The tops were finished with Wolf fur.

Finally the music changed and Nitto appeared in the back of the small Church with standing room only. Beside her stood French. She had chosen him to walk her down the isle. Small Wave stepped out first dressed in traditional Inuit clothing. Her little dress was bright red and trimmed in light blues. Her hair had been brushed and slightly curled. She started up the isle and stopped and talked to people along the way until she saw him and came running. The people all laughed as he scooped her up in his arms. Next came a friend of Nitto's, Kaylil another pretty young Inuit girl, who walked up the isle and stood across from them.

All eyes were on Nitto when she started to slowly walk up the isle. Her dress was white, Caribou leather stained white and beaded with wildflowers. Her hair was tied back in a mass of curls. The smile on her face warmed the whole room. They reached the front and she turned and kissed French. Todd stepped down and took her hand. "You look stunning Nitto. Just as perfect as I knew you would be."

She smiled and they stepped before Pastor Robert. He stood straight and as tall as he could and looked at them both. He spoke in Inuit and Sal stood and translated for his sake.

"We as a community have come together today to be a witness to this marriage. A marriage that has been predestined by God. Nitto and Todd you are about to enter the state of Holy Matrimony in the eyes of God first them to all who are present. The vows that you will repeat this day are vows that are to be held for the remaining days of your lives. It is through this commitment before God that you will live. Could I have you face each other."

Do you Todd take this woman Nitto to be your lawfully wedded wife. To honour and obey, to cherish and care for. To meet all her needs and be the man that God has called you to be as the spiritual leader of the home?

He looked into her eyes and a smile came over her lips. Todd took both her hands into his and said, "I do."

"Do you Nitto take this man Todd to be your lawful husband and agree to honour and obey and love him till death do you part. Do you stand before God and family and friends and accept this commitment to Todd."

Nitto again smiled and said, "I do."

"Now I understand that you have something you would like to speak into each others vows. Speak as you wish and as you do, I ask you exchange rings."

Todd cleared his throat and he was about to speak when Nitto spoke at the same time. They both laughed and the congregation laughed as well. Then it happened a second time and that brought about a round of applause. Sal stepped in and said, "Ok Nitto you first. Todd my boy be quiet."

Nitto took his hands again and stood quietly and then started to speak. "Todd I have waited all of my life for a man to come along and love me the way God has called a man to love a woman. I have been blessed knowing that you have accepted me and Small Wave as yours. I stand here today before God, friends, family and commit myself to be yours completely and fully."

Todd wiped the tears from his eyes. "Nitto in those days when we were isolated together I come to know your heart. It is a heart filled with love of God, creation and all those whom God places in your path. You are a child of the Father above and I stand before Him and the many gathered and pray for wisdom and strength to be the man that God has called me to be. I pledge my love to you this day."

Sal tapped him on the shoulder and passed him a handkerchief. Todd reached over and dabbed Nitto's eyes then his and passed it back to Sal who wiped his as well.

Then Robert spoke again. "We live in a harsh land here Brothers and Sisters. A land that is often unforgiving and yet gives of herself to sustain us. Through all the hardships and pain and suffering come blessings. Blessing such as what we see here today. The blessing of God's love coming full circle by His bringing these two together. By the power vested in me, first by God and then Government of the Northwest Territories I hereby pronounce you husband and wife. Ladies and gentleman Mr and Mrs Todd and Nitto Morris. You may kiss the lovely bride."

Todd took Nitto into his arms and she moulded herself in close to his body. He whispered to her, "May I kiss Mrs Morris like I have always wanted to kiss her?

She blushed and whispered back at him. "You may but just remember we are in public." She smiled. Well we are married now right. Kiss me the way you like."

Todd bent and placed his lips softly on hers and she responded by melting against him.

There was a loud applause as they sat and took their seats. He reached over and took her hand. Pastor Robert preached a sermon on the virtues of marriage and the sanctity of marriage. He directed his instructions to the youth of the community and of the marriage bed remaining pure. He spoke of the blessing that would follow if the steps to remain pure where kept. After he was finished he announced there was to be a gathering at the community centre where there would be much food and entertainment. "Please come and enjoy as we celebrate with Nitto and Todd." He prayed grace over the food and closed by saying. "Thanks be to God for the day He has given."

The remainder of the day and late into the evening was filled with much food, story telling, games and dance. At the end of the night Sal came forward and handed them his Visa card. My gift to you Todd and Nitto is for you to fly south to Texas. Todd I want you to take this lovely lady and introduce her to the many friends you have there at the Mission. I want you to find your family and make peace with them. Here is the address where they are. I hired a private investigator and this is what he found." He passed him an envelope. "I want you to give this to Stan. It is a gift for the work he is doing there. Take the new plane I have bought, it is sitting in Whitehorse. Let me know when you are ready to go and I will fly you. Anything and everything you need will be covered by me."

Todd went to say something and Sal raised his hand. "There is no need to say anything and please do not argue. Son in the top right hand drawer of my desk there is an envelope with your name on it. It is a gift for you but you are not allowed to open it until the time is right. You will know when that is. Now you go in peace and know that you are both dearly loved."

Sal turned and walked slowly away. He had spoken and there was nothing more to be said. Sal walked over and spoke for a minute to Nanapi and passed her an envelope and quietly slipped out the door into the cold night."

At 10 o'clock all who remained gathered around and spoke words of wisdom and love into them. Nanapi took Small Wave by the hand and smiled and spoke in their language. "Tonight is your night, I will care for this child."

With great fan fair a line was formed and they walked through with many well wishers offering small gifts for their journey.

It was 11 when they arrived at Nitto's door and Todd scooped her up in his arms. Well Mrs Morris we are married now, this night has been set aside for us. I want you to know that you have made me the happiest man in the world. I so love you Nitto."

Chapter Thirty Two

"Heading South"

Sal touched down at the Whitehorse airport and smiled as they taxied up to the terminal. "There she is you two. The bright red and white one with the blue lettering. You two will be riding in comfort. I had her painted up special."

Todd sat in awe, the call sign was Tango-Oscar-Delta-Delta 777. "Sal how did you?

"Just by luck and Gods hand I found it. I run a tracer on your call sign from your application and found it was for sale and bought it for you. A man likes to start to rebuild and what a better way than with the familiar. The insurance covered the cost. This can be your little getaway plane for the family. Go in His love and know He travels with you."

Nitto sat somewhat lost with what was happening. Todd was spellbound looking at the plane. He walked around touching it lovingly. Just then he heard the Beaver rev its engines and Sal waved and started to take off. They were left alone again. Todd opened the door and the familiar rich leather smell filled his nostrils. He ran his hands over the seat. He helped Nitto inside and loaded their suitcases and climbed inside running his hands over the controls and turned on the key and fired the first engine then the next. The sound was a sound he could have never forgotten.

Nitto looked concerned. "Nanuq are you ok, you are as white as a ghost?

"Just fine Nitto, this is like a ghost has come back into my life. This plane was my personal plane I had when I owned the business in Texas. I had this built especially for me. Sal has found it and it has come back into my hands again. I have no idea what to say Nitto."

"No need to say anything but thank you Father. This is one of the blessings that Pastor Robert spoke about for living in Gods will Todd. My what a beautiful plane this is. Look at all the detail and the comfort. It is perfect Todd, just perfect."

"Tango-Oscar-Delta-Delta 777, requesting permission to take off. Whitehorse to Calgary then onto Phenix Arizona will be the flight plan."

"You are clear for take off, runway 29, TODD 777. Have a safe flight and congratulations."

"Thank you tower. Could you patch me through to Sal please. He just left in the Beaver."

"Just go ahead Tango-Oscar-Delta-Delta 777 this is an open channel."

"Sal, Nitto and I have no way of thanking you for all your kindness and love."

"All I ask is that you live and love according to Gods will. See you, God willing when you get back. Have fun. Sal over and out."

"Blessings to you Sal. Over and out." Thank you Whitehorse tower. Ready for take off."

Todd pulled out onto the end of the runway, sat for a minute and pushed the throttles full forward. The small plane jumped and in less than 1000 yards they were in the air. He could feel the G force pulling on his face as they climbed. He levelled off at the prescribed 10,000 feet and he settled back."So what do you think?

"We may have to go back so I can get my stomach. Now that was some ride Todd Morris. Still a far cry from our wedding night but this was an experience."

"It was special Nitto our first night. Thank you for being you. This time we have together is going to be special, maybe somewhat painful with the children but in the end fulfilling. I cannot wait to share you with my old friends and my children. They will all love you."

"I hope so Nanuq, I am worried about Sal. Nanapi says she is as well. He gave her a large sum of money the other day and now this, an aircraft and a trip and all?

"I know he told me that he was feeling a little down again the other day and said he thought it was the flu. He seemed fine today though. Very upbeat and his colour was good."

"I know, mind if I pray for him Todd?

"Not at all."

"Father you know the heart Sal has and you know what is happening in his life. If there is something that can be done to heal him that is what we pray for. Thank you for the caring and loving heart he has shown over the years. Bless him Father and keep him safe."

"Amen," Todd added. "Thank you Nitto, that was lovely. Sal will be fine. God will be looking after him."

It was only 11 in the morning when they landed in Calgary Alberta to fuel up and get some coffee and a quick lunch. They had another four hours or so to Phenix. The weather had already started to warm. They walked around the airport a little and looked in a few of the shops.

Nitto spotted a small Polar Bear couple sitting side by side on a log hugging each other. There was no stopping her. She bought them and when they had cleared customs and got back in the plane she set them on the dash. "Perfect."

They again lifted off and were on there way. Calgary had given them clearance straight to Phenix and estimated they would land at 5:20 pm local time. The temperature was 75 degrees above. Todd had booked the bridal suite at an upscale hotel without Nitto knowing. It was a 3 day all inclusive package. They would have no want or need for anything as they would be catered to in style. As they flew they talked about the wedding and the future and what they would do.

"Sal has asked me to stay on and work with him. He says he will slowly step down and allow me to manage the business. He has certainly placed a great deal of trust in me Nitto."

"Rightly so, you have earned his respect. I watched the others come and go that worked for him. They took advantage of him more often than to do him good. Sal has a huge heart and you have done right by him."

"I would like to stay in the North if we could. I love the atmosphere of the people in comparison to people in the south. This will be a good confirmation of what I am talking about coming South and seeing what I left behind."

"You know me Todd I will go anywhere as long as I have peace and love. Thank you for giving that to me.

This will be the first time I have ever gone to the US, so this will be all new to me."

"I hope this is good for you then. I want you to have all you deserve. Sachs Harbour is wonderful. Should you ever want more just say the word and we will start looking."

"We will see Nanuq, she poked the male bear on the dash I would say that you are feeling just fine where you are right now beside your Nitto." She gave a smile and looked at him. "You are more than a man, you are my hero, my lover and my friend. Where you go I will go. It is the way of true love."

Nitto sat in awe of the Grand Canyon as they passed overhead. The land was bare without snow and the deep ravines that had been cut over the years were a stunning contrast. She sat quiet and looked out over the cavernous spaces below. "Oh how I could play down there in those hidden places."

"TODD 777 requesting permission to do some low flying through the grand canyon. We will be in radio contact should we need to change our position."

"Go ahead TODD 777 we have you cleared for 500 feet, Stay within the canyon walls and you will be fine. There is no other traffic at that level."

"Roger 10-4 TODD 777 descending and he moved the yoke fully forward and started to drop from 9500 feet. Nitto hung on for dear life. "Todd Nanuq Morris you are a mad man. You are completely mad. I will be sick soon."

"Think happy thoughts, you wanted to play and play we will. Get ready for the ride of your life." He flipped the plane into a loop and then a roll and he levelled off at 500 feet above the canyon walls.

Nitto laughed, "Mad you are, completely mad."

"Well in that case just open the door and step out and he banked the plane to the right and they were flying with Nitto looking at the ground passing by at high speed. I will box your ears Nanuq if you do not stop this."

Todd laughed and finally levelled off and followed the contour of the canyon walls. They flew several miles and Nitto just smiled. "You are a bad one Todd Morris but I still love you. This is incredible, look at what has been created here."

TODD 777 requesting permission to again assume the 9500 flight path. My passenger has seen enough for today."

Roger roger TODD 777 you are clear to climb and assume 9500. Glad you had a good time."

He again applied full power and pulled back on the yoke and spiralled to the right over and over again until the reached 9500 and he levelled off. Nitto sat with one hand on the dash and one on the roof. She had a grin across her face. "Todd Morris you excite me a great deal. Wait till I get you on the ground I will get even. Now that was something else."

They landed at Phenix International and took a cab to the hotel. Nitto stood in awe of the luxury of the suite. After Todd had tipped the bellman Nitto slipped into his arms. Now Todd Morris my Nanuq of the North I have a few things I need to show you. There is no traffic control here, just God and you and I so you are safe."

Chapter thirty-Three

"Dallas and Beyond"

They had three days of barely moving from the suite located in the penthouse on the 50th floor of the building. The outside afforded them absolute privacy. They were catered to in the finest of style. It was certainly a trip they would be a long while in forgetting.

"Mr and Mrs Morris it has been a pleasure for us to have you as our guests," the manager spoke as they were checking out. I do hope that you have found the service and the facility all that you expected. Please feel free to contact me personally should you ever be in Phenix again."

"Thank you Charles, it has been our pleasure to be here. Everything is more than satisfactory. Could we get a cab to the airport please."

"Please," he waved over a young man. "Peter could you please drive the Morris's to the airport. If they have a little extra time take them where ever they would like to go."

"Very kind of you Charles. We will be sure and recommend your hotel to our associates at the Country Club in Sachs Harbour. They are always looking for adventure and this indeed would be a wonderful place for them to stay. Thank you again."

"We thrive on return business and referrals. Please take a few of my cards and pass them among your membership. Be sure and have them mention your name and I will personally look after all their needs."

The driver took their bags and escorted them to a large black SUV with shaded windows. "Allow me," and Peter opened the door and Todd took Nitto's hand and helped her inside, then climbed in. Peter smiled closed the door and Nitto burst out laughing first.

"Where on earth is there such a place in Sachs Harbour called the Country Club. Oh Nanuq you are a bad one. Can you just imagine all the residents arriving here and checking into this place."

"Yes I can, I can see several of them attempting to fish in the pond in the lobby. If I had the money I would send them all down to enjoy being catered too as we were. I wonder what Charles would do if he only knew about home." They both started laughing.

"Oh Nanuq you crack me up sometime. I can imagine that room cost poor Sal a small fortune?

"Actually I paid for the room. My treat for my dear wife. Afraid you are married to a man who has nothing left to offer. Three nights there cleaned out my savings but I would do that again in a heartbeat for you Nitto."

She looked at him and smiled. "What a wonderful gift Todd, thank you." Then she started laughing again. "It is a good thing to have friends and family to help feed and care for us. I so love living in Sachs compared to what we have just seen. What say we send down a seal or two for Charles and the crew? That started another round of laughing and Todd could see Peter driving and just smiling.

They arrived at the airport and checked into security. They were put through the special screening area set aside for owners of small aircraft and private planes. The guard was an elderly man. "Oh I see you are newly married. Where might you be off to next?

"Dallas and the Fort Worth area to visit with family and friends."

"Well you two travel safe and young man love this lady with all your heart. Life is far too short to be chasing after the dollar all the time. Take it from and older widower that lost his sweetie two years ago. Life is too short."

"Great advice and I can assure you I will be looking after this girl."

"Have a great flight you two. Watching you is like watching me and the Mrs at your age. Please enjoy and go with God and His love."

"We will and may His peace come upon you this day my friend. Thank you for sharing your wisdom and faith."

"Just what we are called to do son. Be blessed."

He did his walk around the plane and climbed in and started the engines. The sound again stirred him inside like it had the first time he had spotted this plane. There was nothing stopping him from buying it. He reached over and put his hand on Nitto's leg. "We are off on another adventure."

"I love adventure with you it has been a long while since I have had so much fun. Are you going to be ok with looking your children up. This may be hard for you, dealing with them and an angry wife?

"I will be fine honey and I want you to be there with me just as we are called to be."

"Of course."

Once he had all the flight plan filed and clearance they pulled into the stacking lane and awaited their turn. "My goodness I have never seen this many planes Nanuq. How do they keep this all straight?

"Just be thankful they do. "Next stop will be Dallas. I think we should rent a vehicle so we can get around. I would like to just walk in on the Mission tonight unannounced. My guess is we will be put to work and then we will be able to visit with all the old crew."

"I will be ready for anything. I have the Lord and you with me. It will be so nice to see all of this world you left behind."

They finally were able to pull out onto the tarmac and he ran through all his checks and applied full throttle. The plane responded and leaped forward. "Oh I so love this power I have missed this so much. Nitto I need to teach you to fly someday. You will love it."

"Sal has taught me about aerodynamics and such over the years, so I have some basic understanding but I have never actually flown before. Is it hard to learn. I so love flying high above the tundra and watching everything pass."

The next half hour he explained the functions of the pedals and the yoke and the way they responded to his touch. "Here take hold of the yoke and place your feet on the pedals and you will feel what happens with each action I do."

Nitto did so and she would smile at the response to each movement. "See it is that easy, now look at the heading here and he tapped the compass. We are on an assigned heading of 162 degrees. Now look at the altimeter it shows we are at 7000 feet." Each time he pointed to something Nitto would lean forward and learn. "Now comes the interesting part. Do you see this small aircraft and this the line that runs horizontal on this gauge. That is called the Attitude Indicator. It is what keeps us level. Look what happens when I tip the wings and start to wonder. The small aircraft leaned to the left. This is what happens when I push the yoke forward, the horizon line drops. The combination of anything I do has an effect on the flight of the aircraft. I suppose the best way to explain it Nitto is what ever you do here changes the way the plane responds. Care to take over for a spell. I will be right here and correct anything you do?

"You have to be kidding me. You want me to fly?

"Why not, I will be right here to help you. Now gently take the controls and I will hang on. When you get off course I will correct you."

"Ok I guess I am ready," and he let the controls go and immediately the plane turned to the right and started to drop. She called out. Todd help me."

"Ok I have it, now lets try again and she took over and the plane started to rise. "Now feel the way the yoke moves when I take control. Watch the Altitude Indicator and fly with it. Just relax and pay attention. It is all yours again."

This time the plane plunged a little and Nitto pulled back and it levelled again. "Very good now turn with the pedals, first to the right then the left and keep and eye on the indicator and compass heading of 162. Very well done." He let go of the yoke slowly. "There you go Nitto you are flying. Simple as that."

"Oh my God Nanuq this is incredible, amazing and out of the world I come from."

"Now you are an official co-pilot. Landing is the hard part. Taking off well that runs a close second. It is all yours for the next hour. Have fun and if you get off course I will let you know."

Nitto sat straight up in the seat, tense and concentrating at the Attitude gauge. Todd could not believe he had been blessed with such a beautiful wife. He reached over and gently ran his hand up and down her back. "You are special Nitto and to think I found you all the way north."

"It has been all my pleasure Nanuq. I love how gentle you are with me."

After about an hour with a few dips and dives he leaned over and kissed her on the cheek. I better take over and get us on the ground so I can show you just how gentle I can be with you."

"Now that sounds interesting." She gave him a smile.

Chapter Thirty Four

"The Mission"

He had called ahead and asked to have a car waiting and for a position to park the plane for a few days. The rental agency was only a few hangers down from where his airlines had been located. His once brightly coloured building was now faded and run down. The terraced flower garden he had designed was an array of weeds. The past was the past. He had a future ahead of him now and he could only focus on a better life.

They had parked the plane and gotten out the suitcases when out of the corner of his eye he caught sight of a lady running toward him. Before he knew it he was holding a very robust Connie Campbell. "Just never know what the heck is going to drop in from above. Would you look at you. If I weren't married Todd Morris I would chase you to the end of time. It is great to see you." Then she planted a big wet kiss on his lips.

"Good to see you Connie, he stood back and looked at her. Still one of the finest looking ladies in Texas."

She stood back and placed both her hands on her hips and laughed. "They make em big in Texas Todd. Now who is this lovely lady, my you are a cutie. Is this big lug trying to take advantage of you honey?

Nitto was a little shocked at Connie and her ways and stumbled for an answer. Todd reached over and pulled her in close. "Connie I would like you to meet Nitto Morris, my wife."

"Oh my, you don't say. Honey you are the sweetest looking little thing I have seen in a long while. Come over here and let Connie greet you Texas style." Before Nitto could move Connie pulled her in and practically lifted her off the ground in a hug. "This here is how we say hello in Texas." She let her go and Nitto stepped in beside Todd. The greeting had been over the top in her world and Todd even sensed some fear and placed an arm around her.

"How are you doing Connie, Jack doing ok?

"Poor Jack is in a home now. That Alzheimer's has taken hold and he is off in his own little world. Horrible disease, robs a person of everything. Me well still trying to hold it all together. Business is slow but has been picking up again. We are praying the economy turns around. Took many good people down with it."

"Sure not the same as the old days Connie is it?

"No certainly not. See that building over there Nitto. That was Todd's once. This man had a flower bed that would turn heads all over. He had the best of the best for aircraft and staff running in all directions. Look at that dump now. I have a complaint into the airport authority and they are trying to get it cleaned up."

"Do you have a car for us Connie?

"Sure do, she placed two fingers in her mouth and whistled catching the attention of an attendant. Get that piece of junk out of here. Bring me my toy, let the man live again."

The attendant waved and Connie turned and looked at him and Nitto. "You two look good together. Todd you are looking the best I have ever seen you. You had us all some scared back then with the addictions and all. I thank God often for keeping you safe. I heard that you were somewhere off the map in Northern Canada?

"We are, Nitto and I live in a place called Sachs Harbour in the Northwest Territories in Canada. I fly for a small company called Midway Air. Just look on the map and it will be close to as far North as you can get."

"Sweetie," she looked at Nitto. "You my dear have one of the finest men to ever come out of Texas. A real gentleman. I am so glad for you two. Look after each other and never forget to tell each other of the love you have. Life can change so fast. I tell that to my Jack now and it is like talking to thin air. Promise to love each other always."

Nitto took a step forward and gave Connie a light kiss on the cheek. "Rest assured we will Connie, it has been wonderful meeting you."

Just then Todd heard the rumble of a motor and out from the hanger came a brand new Cadillac Escalade. Bright red and all shined up. "Connie I can't take this from you?

"Of course you can. I have more insurance on this thing than you can shake a stick at. Just be warned in advance she is a sleeper. That engine has been gone over top to bottom. I use her for drag racing and she has taken trophies all over the State. You see Todd some things never change. I may have a few extra pounds here and there but you know me. I love to live hard and fast when it comes to my vehicles. Enjoy yourself's and you pay for any tickets you get. Good to see you Todd and nice to meet you Nitto."

"Thanks Connie, not all that sure how long we are here for. Watch the plane for us and maybe have Glen do a service on her."

"Wait a minute is that the same plane you had before, you painted it again. That is a firecracker that one. Glen knows it like the back of his hand. He is off today but consider it done and ready when you are."

They took off with the squeal of tires and Connie just laughed and waved as they pulled out. "Now there is quite a lady," Nitto smiled. A little over the top but I like her Todd."

"Connie is a special friend. Her and Jack came in about the same time as I did and they have done well. I used to send allot of business their way and they did the same for me. They are good people."

Todd found his way through traffic and before long it was like the old days. It was something he was used to. Nitto on the other hand was not used to it. They pulled into the parking lot of the Mission at 4:30 and walked in.

Mandy had her back to them and called out. "We are not open till 5, you will need to wait. I have some of the best stew in town."

"What happens if a man is hungry. I suppose you dump garbage all over him."

Mandy stopped working and slowly turned showing a very pregnant lady. A smile broke out over her face and she slowly walked over and looked at Todd. "Would you look at you all cleaned up. What has it been, close to a year now. It is good to see you Too Tall. Think you can get your arms around this one for a hug?

Todd bent and held her close and tears filled their eyes. "Good to see you Short Stuff. Need I ask what happened to you," as he reached down and touched her tummy.

Mandy stepped back, held her tummy and smiled. "Love is what happened, I took your advice and gave Eddy another chance and it was the best thing in the world. Now Too Tall who is this lovely lady?

"This Mandy is Nitto, my wife."

"Now look at you Mrs, you are a very lovely lady. Oh my Todd that is wonderful. You finally found love and had to travel to the end of the world to find it. Short stuff they call me Nitto but it is really Mandy. Todd was one of our stars that made it up through the ranks. A success story that is still talked about. It is nice to meet you."

Nitto gave her a hug. How far gone are you Mandy"

"Eight and a half months. The doctors are saying it could be anytime now. I feel like I am packing a football team in here."

"You look wonderful, is this the first?

"It is and to think this was never suppose to happen. I was considered to be barren."

Just then a voice came from behind them. "I had enough in me to change that Mandy. All you needed was one little egg and the rest well just happened. My God would you look who has come back to say hello. Good to see you again Todd."

He stuck out his hand. "Good to see you again Eddy, you are looking good my friend."

"Todd I owe you a debt of gratitude for sending my girl back."

"It was meant to be. Eddy this is Nitto my wife. Eddie here gave me a hand up with all the warm clothes I came North with. Good to see you Eddy. Do you still have the store?

"I do but we have moved it all in the back and just give it all away now. Stan and I made a deal and this is how I pay the rent in serving."

"Is Stan around?

"He is in the back office. Just go back, we need to finish up here. You will stay for dinner with us?

"Better than that we will help."

They walked through the back to the very far corner of the building. A dim light spilled out into the hallway. "What does a man have to do to get a meal around here for a couple of lonely lost travellers?

"Just be here is all." Stan stood and looked over his reading glasses. "My Lord would you look who has come back. Todd Morris, I still have your post card hanging on the bulletin out front. Come in here and let me have a look at you."

They stepped in and Stan looked at Nitto. "Oh my I see that you have brought a friend, an angel. Stan Ramsey and you are?

"Mrs Nitto Morris. I have heard much about you and the work you are doing here. Thank you for saving my husband Stan."

"Congratulations, my I see there have been some real improvements. Sit please. It is so good to see you. Are you still in the North flying with," He paused. "My memory is failing me lately?

"Sal Preston of Midway Air. Yes still there and loving the North Stan. You are looking well?

"I have slowed Todd. A medical thing and they can do little for me. Lou Garrick disease they say. I have a few years left I can do this then I have to step back. Eddy and Mandy are training to take over."

"So sorry to hear Stan."

"It is life and if it is God's will well then it is just that. The mission is struggling some and still trying to come out of the recession. America has been hit hard and our numbers of feeding have tripled since you were here. But at the end of the day God provides."

"He does Stan. Here is a little something that Sal asked me to pass along." He passed him the envelope and Stan looked at it.

"What on earth is this. I only spoke to the man a few times on the phone."

"Not that sure, I know I spent a fair amount of time sharing with Sal what you are doing here. I guess he felt a little something would come in handy."

Stan opened the envelope and read a small handwritten note then looked at the check and his eyes opened wide. He looked up and began to weep. "Here look at this Todd and tell me again that God provides." He passed over the check and it was made out to the Mission and the total was for 50,000 dollars. He passed over the note and they read Sals handwriting.

"Just a little seed money to help you along and my way of saying thank you for saving Todd. Do His work my friend."

Todd and Nitto could only smile. This small quiet man in the far north had blessed another with such a gift. Stan wept and prayed for Sal and his kindness. "Thank You Father for all Your servants."

Chapter Thirty Five

"Dinner and Rest"

They stayed for dinner that night and helped out getting ready for the morning rush before Todd stood and said. "We really do have to get on the road, just so you all know I will be seeing my children again tomorrow. Thank you for all your care and support. Say hello to all the crew at the treatment centre for me. Tell them I will stop around and say hello if I get a chance. Love all of you."

After all the goodbyes they promised to stay in touch. They drove to the outskirts and found a nice hotel and took a room for the night. After they were all checked in Nitto ran the tub. "Could I get a man to wash my back?

"No need to ask twice my lady, your wish is my command."

"Really I was looking at the tub and it is very big. Maybe you could join me and I could wash your back as well."

"I think we need to test it out. Race you," and he started to take his clothes off and was in the tub first.

"Hardly fair Nanuq. You know that I am still shy and modest."

"That will change. Come along and I will take away all that shyness. You are lovely and no need to hide from me."

She reached over and shut off the light, only the light from the room filtered into the bathroom. She slowly took off her clothes and lay back onto his chest. "Thank you for being patient with me."

"Of course," and they lay talking of the day and he slowly washed her back. The rest of the night was spent in quiet, gentle lovemaking.

The following morning they arose. She came in close to him and hugged him. "Another amazing night with my Nanuq. Are you going to be ok today, this may be hard for you. Just know that I stand with you dear."

"I know. God has given a helper according to what He teaches in the Bible. I know that I have a helper in you. I will be fine honey. Come along and lets see what the day brings about."

They drove to the address in Fort Worth that Sal had the investigator find. The closer they got the more run down the district became. They ended up in front of a run down house with a lawn that was poorly kept. There was an older model car standing in the driveway with the hood up and a flat tire. He checked the address again and said."I guess this must be it. My lord what has become of my family."

Todd stood and helped her out of the vehicle and started to walk towards the house. A man stepped outside with a cigarette in his mouth and a can of beer in his hand. "If your looking for money there is none here. The welfare gets here next week. So might as well just move along."

"I am looking for Marie Morris?

"Never heard of her, I have an old lady named Marie but the Morris part I have no idea what you are talking about. If you want you can take her with you. Dried up old hag anyway. Had about all I can take from her whining and complaining."

"Maybe you could tell me where Linsey and Jeff are?

The man took a menacing step off the front porch and turned a little sideways. Todd took Nitto and made her stand back as he approached. He stopped a few feet in front of the man. "I am their father and I would like to see my children."

Just then the screen door slammed shut. "It was Marie or what was left of her. She had gained a considerable amount of weight, her face was drawn and her hair a mess. She carried a half empty bottle of wine. "Well would you look who the cat drug back from the dead. Sidney, this is the jerk that beat me all the time, maybe he needs a lesson or two. What say you clean his clock for him, just remind him it is a man he is against this time and not a lady like me."

Todd looked at the man in front of him. He drank back the rest of his beer, burped a loud belch and crushed the can in his hand and tossed it down. "Always ready for a good scrap, beating on the ladies are you. Come along man lets mix it up a little. He made a lunge with his right hand and Todd stepped aside. Sidney stumbled and looked at Nitto. Maybe I should hang a licking on your lady like you did mine Pal."

Sidney took one step toward Nitto and it was the last step he took. Todd grabbed him and as he swung around Todd connected him square in the face with a blow that sent him into a heap on the ground. Marie started screaming and threatened to call the police.

"I have come to see my children, from what I see here this is deplorable and my children deserve better than this. Marie I will do all in my power to get my children back. If you plan on fighting me on this then I suggest you get cleaned up because this will be fast and just. You had your way once and I will not allow it to happen again. I have rights as a father and it is my right to say this is all wrong. What on earth happened to you, look at you Marie, you are disgusting.

"Take the damned children, all they have been is a millstone around my neck anyway. They will be here soon. Pack them up I have had enough of them anyway. I have always hated them because they loved you more anyway. Look there they are now. Look at that tart you have for a daughter, dressed like a hooker and your son look at him. Thinks he is some kind of jock or something. Take the two of them and let me die in peace."

Todd could not hear her anymore as he looked at his children. Linsey was short like her mother. Her dress was short but she looked neat. She looked at her dad and started to run towards him and stopped. She looked again and when he smiled she ran into his arms. "Daddy, Daddy I knew that you would come back for us. I love you and I miss you so much." She kissed him all over his face.

Next came Jeff. He slowly walked up to his dad and stood and finally smiled. "You are the Dad I have been praying would come back. Look at you Dad you are all better." He held back his tears as long as he could then took both his children into his arms and they all cried.

"Children I would like you to meet someone who is very special to me. Linsey and Jeff this is my wife Nitto. We have only been married a short while. We are now living in a place called Sachs Harbour in the Northwest Territories in Canada."

Nitto moved in close and smiled. I have heard much about you two. Your Dad has talked of you many times. What a pleasure to finally meet you."

They both stepped forward and were very polite. The moment was lost when a bottle crashed at their feet. Marie had thrown it. "Get these stupid kids out of my life. I am tired of looking after the likes of them. All they ever talk about is you anyway. Get in here and pack what they want." She looked at her own children and spat out the words. "I hate both of you."

They stepped past who was sitting on the ground getting his bearings. His nose was off to one side with blood running down his chin and onto his stained shirt. "Might want to stay right there Mr. Try anything and trust me there is more where the last one came from."

"Come along children, lets get you away from all of this. We will work this all out after." He led them into the house. Each room they passed was filled with filth and empty bottles. There were injection rigs laying on the table and bags of drugs on the counter.

Marie turned on Nitto and started to call her names. "You must be his new whore. Ya! You look like one, some damned squaw he found in the north. Look at you all miss high and mighty. Bet you will never be as good as me sister."

Nitto turned and faced her. "How dare you call me such things lady. You known nothing about me or my people. How dare you," She gave Marie a push and sent her flying back into a chair in the corner. "You sit there and shut up before I teach you a little Inuit justice." She pointed her finger at her. "One more word from you and I will unleash some fury on you like you have never seen before. Now shut up and let Todd and the children clear out of this dump." She found a piece of paper and wrote out an agreement that stated Todd had the right to take the children under his care. The last line stated I agree that I am an unfit mother and want them to have a decent home with Todd Morris.

"Here sign this now before I get angry and trust me lady you would never want to anger me."

Marie started to read and Nitto hollered "Sign it. All it says is that you agree to allow Todd to take the children. Sign it or I will make you sign it."

Marie bent and gave it a sprawling signature signing away her right. "There you tramp, now you can raise them."

Todd and the children walked out and stopped. The children looked at their mom sitting in the chair. The look in their eyes was one of pity. She was but a shell of who she was before. She reached for the drugs and the last thing they saw was her heating a spoon and injecting herself. Her last words were "Bastards, go back to your bastard father. May you all rot in hell."

After they had settled into the hotel and were having supper Todd filled his children into what had taken place in his life. "I have no idea what you have been through Linsey and Jeff but from what I have seen today I can imagine it has not been good. I want you to know that all of that is in your past."

Linsey took Jeff's hands in hers. "Dad you will never know. We have prayed together all this time that you would return and look our prayers have been answered. Thank you for coming. This is the lowest we have seen mom. Is there anything we can do to help."

"Children only if she is willing. I have no idea where this will all go. I remember you like snow, if you are willing I would like to take you to a land of snow, ice and a completely different lifestyle. We can make this work. Nitto and I have a daughter who is 10 her name is Small Wave and is in need of a sister and brother. Do you think you could fill those shoes. It is very cold there but I can tell you the people are real and caring."

"Dad we will go anywhere with you, Nitto and yes Small Wave. Please take us away from all of this and love us like you used too."

"I have never stopped loving you children. Never, we will make this work."

After they had the children settled in Todd called Sal. "Sal how are you?

"Doing well Todd, how are you and the Mrs doing. God man I miss you here. I have more freight than you can shake a stick at. I had to hire French's young son to help. Still fighting that flu bug. Doc says I am getting old. Can you imagine. What is up son?

"Sal I found my children and things are not good. I want to bring them North. Do you think I can put them in the trailer for the time being until we sort through everything?

"Todd you bring them home and we will get it all worked out, never you mind about anything. God always has a greater plan in the end."

"Thanks Sal, I miss you brother."

"Man I tell you Todd. I know now the value of having you around."

"I will be back soon Sal, hang in there, Stan says God Bless you for the gift. I might add that is some gift my friend."

"Just wanted to make sure it went to a good cause is all. See you when you get here. How is Nitto and the plane?

"Both are amazing. Nitto even tried some flying and has the touch, she sends her love. Say hello to Nanapi and Small Wave from us. We will see you soon my friend. God Bless Sal."

"Blessing to you, now I need to get some shut eye. Love you son."

Chapter Thirty Six

"Getting all in Order"

Todd placed another call to his longtime friend and attorney Bill Stinson at his home number. Bill had been his attorney for many years and through the crash of his company. The phone rang several times and finally Bill answered the phone. "Bill Stinson speaking, how may I help you?

"Bill it is Todd Morris calling. It has been a long while. Sorry for calling you at home but I have a question I would like to ask if you are not busy?

"Todd what a wonderful surprise, last I heard you were being carted off to prison. Gail at the office told me she heard you were working up in the far North somewhere?

"All true. Bill do you recall I had a court order to stay away from Marie and the kids after I got out of prison? It expired last month and through a friend and his investigator I found Marie. The children were living in terrible conditions so I pulled them out and have them here with me. Their mother is a drug addict and she signed a paper today authorizing me to take them. Is there a chance we could meet tomorrow and discuss or nextstep in me obtaining custody?

"Of course Todd. I will be in the office at 9. Just come over and have Gail call me. The door is open for you always. I did hear that Marie had really slipped. What a shame. Tell me Todd are you ok, I mean with the addictions and all."

"Doing great Bill. I will be around in the morning."

Next he called the Fort Worth Police Department and reported the condition of the home and the fact that there were drugs in the home. He gave the officer the address, the deputy on the other end of the line sounded disinterested. "Unless they are dealing the stuff, it's not likely the matter will be looked into."

"In that case I think you had better because it looked to me like there was some very suspicious activity taking place with minors involved."

"How can you be reached if we need to speak to you again. Could I get your name please?

"The name is Todd Morris and I can be reached through my attorney Bill Stinson. He will know where to locate me. The minors are my children and I have them in my care."

"Very well, thank you for letting us know. Is there anything else I can help you with Mr Morris?

"Yes actually there is Dan Butler still the Chief there?The tone of the officer changed somewhat. "

"Yes Sir he is, he is in tonight would you like to speak with him."

"Please I know Dan will look into this matter immediately." The phone went silent. Then came the deep voice of the Chief.

"Well would you look who has turned up again. Morris you old dog it has been a long while. Lets see, Oh that is right. Not the best circumstance the last time we met. How are you doing my friend?

"Doing better than the last time we chatted. How is Veronica and the kids?

"All doing well. Kids man where have you been. Danny was married two years ago and I am now a Gramps. It has been a long while. I hear that you are flying in the North. How are Linsey and Jeff doing?

"The reason I called Dan. Marie really fell off the deep end, into some drugs, hard stuff. She was shooting it up today. She is living with a real piece of work. I stopped today to see the kids and afraid it got ugly. I had to defend myself and the whole thing exploded and I have the children with me. I could not leave them there in those conditions. I called in and gave the address to the officer that contacted you. Any chance I could have you check in. Afraid that place will not be a happy home once she comes down off her high."

"Of course man. Give me the address again and I will have the boys do a check. Matter of fact Todd I will do it myself."

Todd read off the address. "Oh, that place. Yes we are aware of it. Are you saying that Marie is tied in with that low life. We have had many a run in with him and his crew."

"She is, thanks Dan. If you need me you can reach me here at this number or through Bill Stinson. I will be meeting him tomorrow to get the custody all in order. The children's welfare is at stake and they will not be going back there again."

"I understand Todd. Love them man. I will call and let you know what is happening. Did you see any weapons at the house?

"I was inside but my only concern was to get the kids out. Sorry I did not look around much. I did notice a few pieces of dark wood behind the front door. They may have been gun stocks but hard to say."

"Thanks I will take a few units with me. Take care friend. Good to hear from you. Maybe a coffee after this all settles down."

He slipped across the hall to the room he had gotten for his children. He leaned against the door jam and watched Nitto holding Linsey close and Jeff was on his knees giving comfort. Nitto looked up and smiled. "We are just getting to know each other Nanuq. You have some wonderful children here."

They both stood and came to him at the same time. Linsey continued to cry as he took them both into his arms. "We will be alright children, I have everything legally started. You always have been and always will be my children. What you have been through has come to an end. I promise you that you will never have to go back and see that again. Never."

Nitto stood and slipped in under his arm. It was touching to watch as this big yet gentle man held his wife and two children and wept. The nightmare for them was over.

Chapter Thirty Seven

"New Everything"

Over breakfast the following morning Todd explained the process of the legal system to them and what had to take place in order for them to come North legally. "I will be meeting with my Attorney this morning to get things started."

"Nitto could you take these two and buy them both some new clothes. There is a mall across the street that caters to all ages. You two get what ever you want. We can stop once we get further into Canada and get some winter clothes. It is time that I started being a proper dad again." He slipped Nitto his own personal credit card. "I will be back after this meeting and maybe we can all take in a movie and have a late dinner. It is so special to see you both again. Linsey and Jeff I am so proud of you for staying together through all of this. I am going to see about getting your mom some help as well. I have some friends that may be able to step in. They are the same ones that helped me and do some wonderful work."

Linsey spoke softly. "Dad why would you do that for mom after all she has done to us. I mean she was the one that started all this mess."

"No Honey it was me. You see I started using drugs and with the economy and all it caused this, mainly my fault and I take the blame. Please honey do not blame your mom for all of this. She will always be your mom. The things you heard yesterday Linsey and Jeff were coming from an addict without a hope in life. Just pray for God to intervene and help her."

Nitto smiled and placed a hand on his arm. "You go do what you have too Nanuq and I will look after all the shopping."

Jeff looked at her. "Nanuq," what does that mean?

Todd laughed. "It is a name the Inuit have given to me. It means Big Polar Bear." You see all white people get traditional names. Wait if all this works out you two will have them as well."

Todd stepped into the spacious office where Bill had his law firm. The interior was very expensive looking. Fine woods from all over the world and expensive pieces of artwork and modern sculptures. He was bent over one when someone pinched his bottom. "Gail I am a married man. You had better stop that."

"Ya need a little honk once in a while Todd. When you reach our age that is all that is left anyway. Let me have a look at you big fella. My look at the tan and the weathered look you have. I hear that you are some kind of maverick bush pilot now?

"You might say that. Come here you sweet young thing and give me a proper hug."

"Oh my she said as she touched her greying hair. Can you say that again. Been a long while since anyone called me young." They both laughed.

Bill stepped out of his office. "I see you two are at it again. Todd you should have married this one years ago. Look at her, she is always dressed in the finest and will always be my babe on the side."

"Liar, Liar, oh my how flattering this is, two good looking men trying to get my attention. Just keep them coming. I will bring you in coffee, just making a fresh pot. Still black Todd if I recall?

"Yes Gail, thank you and always know that I will love you more than this guy will."

"Todd Morris, it is good to see you again. Come in and fill me in on all that you know about this terrible thing that has happened to Marie."

A few hours later Bill had all the papers drawn up. I think this will be fairly clean cut and dried Todd. You have without a doubt proven your fit to be a father again. I will call Dan and see what he has learned. I have a judge friend that deals in family court and I think we can have this wrapped up in a few days."

"I have no idea how I can repay you Bill for all of this. I make little money. Send me a bill and I will whittle away at it over time."

"Tell you what Todd. Slip the extra into a trust fund for the children and we will call it square. Back in the early days when I was starting out it was your firm and a few others that built all of this. It is my way of saying thank you. My services will always be free to a fellow Christian brother. God bless you."

"Thank you Bill. You can reach me at this number when this is all wrapped up. I told Chief Dan Butler he can reach me through you as well."

He went back to the hotel and found he had some time on his hands and placed a call to Chief Butler. "Hi Todd, I was about to call you and let you know what all has taken place. I have some sad news Todd."

"Well might as well tell me now. The children are out with my wife Nitto, so tell it up straight Dan."

"Sidney Crossly is dead. When we arrived he stepped out with a shotgun and fired at one of the officers. We had no choice but to take him down. Marie is in bad shape. She is in ICU at Fort Worth General. When we found her she had a needle hanging from her arm. She overdosed but is still alive. They have her on life support. She is not expected to live Todd. Sorry to be the one to tell you man. I will leave it with you if you want to take the children to see her. Legally they have to keep her alive until a family member comes and authorizes her to be taken off support. I mentioned you and the State says that you cannot make that choice because you are divorced. Do you know if she had family?

"A brother in Tucson is all I know of. Chuck Reeves. The last I heard he was still alive. He lived in some low cost housing in the downtown area. That is about all I know."

"Well its a start anyway. Man she is some rough looking Todd compared to the old days. Marie was one fine looking lady a few years back."

"Yes she was. The years have taken their toll. I will talk to the kids when they get back. Thanks for the update Dan. Say hi to the family. Maybe next time we come down we can come around for a visit?

"It would be nice Todd. Take care my friend. I will be in touch if anything changes."

It was close to four in the afternoon when Nitto and the children arrived. They were loaded down with packages and bags of clothes and personal items. Linsey jumped into his arms. Jeff slapped him on the back. "Thanks Dad for all the neat stuff he said and sat on the couch beside Nitto. You have the coolest wife that anyone could ask for."

Linsey put her arms around his neck and kissed him. "Dad we have missed you. All those things about you that Mom said were not true. You never did leave us. Nitto tells us that you could not because Mom filed a court order against you. Is that true Dad?

"It is Linsey and not sure what your mom said about me. It does not matter anyway because that is all in the past. Sit I have something I want to talk to you about."

Todd bent his head and then explained what Dan had said to him. "The choice is yours, if you would like to visit her or not. I can drive you over. Personally I think you should so you can have some closure. They are saying that she is on life support now and it is not looking good."

Linsey looked at Jeff and the reality of life came to them both. "Dad we would like to see her and at least say goodbye."

"Now you see what I mean about forgiveness children. Good for you. Lets drive over there now and do the right thing. Nitto would you like to come along?

"Todd this is a family thing and I think a time for you and the children. I will stay behind and have a long bath. You go and do what needs to be done. I will be praying for all of you."

They arrived at the hospital and were escorted into ICU. Marie lay with tubes and electrodes attached to her. Her breathing was mechanical. Her colour was grey. The children were solemn and yet knew what this meant. He left them alone with her. The head nurse stopped him in the hall. "Her brother called and said she would not want to live like this. He has faxed us an order to disconnect her from all support. After you leave Mr Morris we will remove her from life support. If you would like to stay you can. We are so sorry."

Chapter Thirty Eight

"Heading North Again

The papers had all been filed. Linsey and Jeff were his again and the buzz from the back of the plane told him all was well with them. They were happy to be heading somewhere other than where they had come from. Their mother had passed away a few minutes after they had left and he shared with them she had. They had shed a few tears. It was over and they were off to a new life. Jeff had bought some maps and a few books and was busy reading. Linsey was talking to Nitto and asking all about her people. Yes life was good and Todd just sat and smiled. They were heading home again.

They stopped again in Calgary and stayed overnight. They took a cab and bought some winter clothes for the children. They were excited about snow. It was something they had never seen in person, only on TV and the movies. Calgary only had a skiff of snow but they were excited.

The following morning they were on their way to the final leg of their journey. Nitto looked over at him and smiled. "You look tired Todd, would you like me to take over again? She cocked her head off to one side and smiled.

"Of course my dear. I know you have been itching to get at the controls. Today I want you to sit back like me and just relax. Do the same as you did the other day but relax." Nitto took over the controls and was flying again after a few dips and left and right turns. "That is better, now just relax and do not fight the plane. Very good. You are a natural at this."

Jeff leaned forward. "You mean to say that Nitto is flying the plane. Man that is cool. Do you think you could teach me Dad?

"Of course Son, we can do anything as long as we are family. We still have a few hours before we get home. I see that we have lots of snow on the ground the further North we head. Look at the tops of the mountains they are covered. Do you two think you are ready for this. This will be the coldest you have ever seen?

"Like you said Dad we are family. This is so cool. What are we gong to do about school?

Nitto smiled. I will be your teacher. I homeschool Small Wave already and I can take over teaching you what you need." She smiled. "Well maybe you can teach me somethings as well. It has been a long while since I attended school."

A few hours later Sachs Harbour came into view. "There we are everyone. That is home up ahead. TODD 777 do you copy Yellowknife. Requesting landing at Sachs."

Then came some static. Roger TODD 777 you are clear to land. Good to have you home again Todd. Say hello to Sal for us."

"Roger will do." They made a long sweeping pass over the hamlet then came back in for a landing. Sal stepped out of the hanger and hobbled over just when Todd opened the door.

"Good to see you Todd. I see that you have brought the family and this sweet young wife of yours back all safe and sound."

"I have. Sal this is Linsey and Jeff. Sal here is my boss."

Sal smiled."No I am your Dads partner. You see we run this thing we call an airline together. Welcome to you both. I hope you like this place as much as your dad here. A fine man he is."

Nitto smiled and slipped over and gave Sal a hug. "Good to see you again Sal. I missed you. Better look out Todd here they come."

He turned and many from the community came to meet them. Each patted him on the back. The younger ones stood back a little and only smiled at Linsey and Jeff. Then Small Wave came running and jumped into her moms arms. They chatted away in their language then she introduced her to the children. Jeff knelt and Small Wave placed her arms around his neck and kissed him on the cheek. Linsey did the same and Small Wave ran her fingers over her face and said, "Pretty." They all laughed then she reached for Todd and he picked her up and tossed her in the air and caught her again. She took his face in her little hands looked at him and smiled. "Small Wave love Dad."

"Yes and Dad love Small Wave."

Nanapi came forward and smiled and took both Linsey and Jeff's hands and started to walk back towards town. "Eat," she said. All they could do was follow.

"You go Nitto and be with them. I will get the bags and put the plane away." She hesitated. "Go sweetie I will be along shortly."

Sal brought the ATV around and they loaded all they had. Todd started the plane and ran it close to the doors and Sal opened them. They pushed the plane inside and parked it.

"How are you feeling Sal?

"Been better Todd. Good to have you home. Really missed you son."

"Missed you as well. Sal I have run up some hefty bills on your credit card. You can deduct it off of my payroll."

"No I will let you do that. Come to my office I have something I need you to sign." He led the way and Sal slid some papers across to him. It was an agreement making him a full partner in the business.

"Sal I can't accept this. This what you have here is a whole lifetime of work. I have nothing to offer as a partner."

"Yes you do Todd my boy. You see you are the son I never had, you have all the qualities I would want in a son. You know the Lord, you married into the community, you have a family now and anyway I just plain love you. Lets call this a wedding gift from me to you. Do we have a deal or do I need to bring in a new pilot?

"Sal this is far to generous. I did not expect this."

"Well you earned it. Now sign the darn paper so I can fax it off in the morning. That will make you a full partner in the business. That way I won't have to pay you all that overtime catching up on the freight I have piled in the back. Please Todd just sign."

Todd looked at him and bent and signed the papers. He took Sal and gave him a hug. "This means a great deal to me Sal. God Bless you for this."

"Trust me son, He already has many times over during my years here in the North. Now get over and be with your family. The trailer is all ready for the kids. I had a new bed brought in so at least they have their privacy till you get this all sorted out. I think Nitto will have to have a new home built by the Government. Being Native she can do that Todd. Something you may want to talk about. Having family separated is not what God wants. Now get out of here and know that I love you son."

Chapter Thirty Nine

"Different Lives"

Todd walked slowly back down to Nanapi's home along the sea shore. Even though it was cold outside he had a sense of urgency rising inside of him. He prayed about it as he sat on an overturned boat and looked out at the ending day. There was a feeling deep inside he was not quite able to put his finger on. Maybe it was all this newness and change. Now married to Nitto with the responsibility of having three children to care for, plus the fact that he was now a full partner in the business. Life had changed from his first days at the Mission.

The closer he approached to Nanapi's home the more he felt what he was doing was right. He stopped and looked inside the window. Jeff was sitting on a chair playing an Inuit game with Small Wave. Linsey was watching Nanapi work on some beading. Nanapi was encouraging her to try. Linsey took the needle and hide and ran the thread through and back up again and pricked her finger. Nanapi laughed and that started all of them laughing.

Nitto looked up at him standing at the window and smiled. "What more could a man be asking for," he spoke aloud to God. "Let Thy will be done and not mine."

He stepped in and took off his parka and boots. The table had been set and steaming bowls of soup and fresh bannock was on the table. Hands were extended and he prayed grace over the meal. He wept at the many blessings that had been brought his way.

Later that night he walked Linsey and Jeff back to the trailer. "It is not much but at least it is warm and dry. We will work something out once we get our bearings again."

"Dad," Linsey spoke. "No matter where we are we are together and that is all that counts. Now if you can do something about all this snow and cold we would be very happy."

Jeff poked his sister. "Come on Lin, we are Northerners now and Nanapi says we are not to whine. Just get used to it is all she said." He laughed come on now smile cause I love you. Compare this to where we came from and tell me where you would rather be?

Todd opened the door and found all had been made ready. The fridge had been stocked with supplies. A bed sat in what was once the living room and a curtain had been installed. Todd took Linsey to her room down the hall. "This will be yours for the time being honey, Jeff you can bunk out in the living room. If you need me all you have to do is use this radio and call me. I have one at the house. You two will be just fine."

Both Linsey and Jeff moved in close to their dad as he prayed over them. Jeff smiled and looked up at his dad. "Just like the old days, you know you praying for us each night."

"It is son. I want you both to know that I have never stopped praying for you. This is an extreme change from where you came from but we are together and that is all that counts. Nitto and I will do everything we can to make a home so we can all be together. I promise you."

Linsey looked up at her dad and smiled. "Dad I really think Nitto is beautiful and I do like your friends. Thank you for coming back and taking us away. We love you."

"And we all love you two as well. Now get some rest. I see there is food and everything so consider this to be your own home for the time being. I will come around in the morning and see how you are doing."

Todd walked back to his own home looking back at the small trailer. This was a real adventure for Linsey and Jeff. There would be many changes coming over the next while.

Nitto was waiting for him when he stepped into the small home. She had a large binder open in her lap. She lifted her head and smiled. "Todd a family is never complete until they are all under one roof. You do know that the Government provides housing for us Inuit. It is part of our treaty and traditional right. The housing is provided upon request. Come and look at the options with me. I want us all to be together."

Todd made two cups of tea and sat with her at the kitchen table. The homes were modular. They would be barged in and assembled on site. The floor plans varied. A few hours later they had one they both liked. It was a simple layout and had four bedrooms. "There I think that is the one for us Todd Morris. Now tell me what does it feel like to be an Inuit man?

He laughed. "This is all new to me Nitto, I mean I have always had to buy my homes or build them."

"There are many benefits Todd. Our children have all their educations paid for including College or University."

"I should get you a booklet that tells all which is provided. Did you know that I will even be paid a small fee for teaching all the children. We will need to take Linsey and Jeff over to Yellowknife to be tested to see where they stand education wise."

"There is also some funding available to help get them proper winter wear. I have a friend in Yellowknife that is a wiz at getting all the paperwork done. Maybe you can take us all on a date next week and we can do this all at once?

"Deal, I like our dates. I promise this time to keep the plane in the air."

"Now I like that plan. We can go to the Indian Affairs Office and get you and the children registered for all the Treaty rights and at the same time order our new home. It can all be done at the same office."

"As simple as that, any chance a man could cuddle with the sweetest girl in Sachs Harbour. I could show her just how much I love her."

She jumped up just out of his reach. "Maybe we should order a five bedroom home Nanuq just in case," and ran to the bedroom.

Todd shut off the lights checked in on Small Wave and slipped into bed beside his wife. She cuddled in close and they both fell asleep. They were home again."

Chapter Forty

"Changes and Blessings"

Todd set a business card Sal had made up for him down on the table in front of Nitto. It read Todd Morris, Partner and Managing Director of Operations."

Nitto picked up the card and read it again and looked at him with a puzzled look. "What does this mean Todd?

"Simply that I have become a full partner in Midway Air. Sal called me into the office the night we came back and gave me the offer and had me sign the official documents. I or shall I say we now own half of Midway Air Nitto."

She looked in shock, then jumped up and gave him a long hug. "Oh Nanuq I am so proud of you. Your hard work and dedication to Sal has come back many times over. What can we do to show Sal our appreciation?

"I would like to take as much work as I can off his hands. I am very concerned about his health. He is coughing badly and constantly holding his chest. We have a flight over to Yellowknife tomorrow and I intend on taking him to a doctor there. His argument will mean nothing. This time he will get a full checkup. I can get the kids helping with sorting and loading freight."

"Maybe we can take today in that case and take care of all this housing and get the kids tested and do a little shopping. We do s few things anyway?

"Be a good day, Sal said yesterday that I should take a day or two and get life back in order. I will slip up and see that the kids are ok this morning. I will let Sal know we are taking the day to slip over and take care of things in Yellowknife. Be ready say in an hour. This will be a fun day as a family."

Todd stopped and found the kids were up already. Linsey had made breakfast and they were just cleaning up. "I see that you have settled in alright. We are taking a flight over to the city of Yellowknife today. We need to take care of some business and have you guys tested to see where you are in your education. Nitto has agreed to home school you."

"Awesome, Jeff smiled. Linsey just teased him and he blushed."

"Dad I think your son has fallen head over heels with your beautiful wife." She laughed.

Todd took his son in his arms and roughed his hair. I better watch out that you do not steal her from me."

Jeff jostled with his dad. "Na I just think she is beautiful is all dad and love the way you and her are so close. It is special to see after what we have watched the last few years."

"I understand son. Can you be ready in an hour. I will get the plane ready. Nitto and Small Wave will be coming along today. It will be a family day and I think we will be able to find some fast food place for you two."

Linsey smiled. "Dad we are both careful what we eat, so just regular food is good enough."

"Good to hear. Meet you at the hanger in an hour. I need to talk to Sal anyway. Love you both. We are going to be getting you some real winter clothes today as well. See you in a little while."

"Sal how are you doing this morning?

"Oh you know," he laughed. Still alive the last time I checked."

"That is a good thing. Are we all set for tomorrow. Get all the freight back so I can go to work?

"Looking forward to flying with you again. That old girl is running like a top. I would like to leave early so be here at 6 in the morning."

"Will do and Sal book yourself and appointment at the clinic." He pointed a finger at him. "No excuses I want you in there to get a complete checkup. That is the rule or you are grounded till you do. I want to make sure and look after my new partner. I want you around for a long while yet."

"Ya, Ya I know. This is like being married to you Todd. Ok lets get things looked at while we are there."

"Good. Sal I will be taking the family over to Yellowknife today. Mind if I take the Hot Rod?

"Half yours now pal, just fine with me. Better ask the other guy," and he pointed at Todd. "How did she fly son?

"Like a dream. I still can not believe that you found her after all this time."

"Pays to be connected son. Trust in the Lord and He will always lead you in the right direction. Good to see that you have all the family together. Man is not meant to live alone. Maybe I should find me another." He grinned.

Twenty minutes later they were in the air and on there way. Todd flew at 1000 feet the entire way so everyone could get a good look at the lay of the land. He pointed out lakes with names and before long Yellowknife came into view. The tower gave him clearance to land and he rented a vehicle and they made all the stops.

First being at the Indian Affairs office. Nitto produced their marriage licence and they were filed under the Indian Act as married. He and Linsey and Jeff were photographed and issued with what was called a Treaty Card. It would allow them to buy anything without having to pay taxes. Next they visited the housing office and Nitto explained to them the need for a new and larger home and they checked their qualifications and the home was ordered. It was as simple as that. Todd was amazed at the system the Canadian Government had in place to look after natives. Next was the testing office for the Board of Education and both Jeff and Linsey passed with very high averages and a course outlined was designed for them. Again all of this was taken care of by the Government.

They found a family restaurant downtown and ordered their meals. Nitto cuddled in close to Todd. "So Nanuq how does it feel to be a Inuit Native?

He laughed. "I can not believe the system that you have in place here for the natives in comparison to what they face in the US."

"Well I have heard but by marrying me you will never have a thing to worry about." She looked at the children all talking and attempting to communicate with Small Wave. "I would say that we are all going to be blessed. Small Wave sat with me this morning and we had a long chat about being a family. My little girl is growing up quickly Todd."

"This will be good for Linsey and Jeff as well. I just pray they integrate well into the community. Linsey has always been a little bit of a socialite like her mom and Jeff well into the sports and all."

"Nanapi is very taken by Linsey and how quick she has picked up on beading. There are many young girls in Sachs that will help guide her. Jeff will learn some of the Inuit sports and will do just fine. God will look after all the details Todd. Have no fear, after all He has looked after us."

"What happens to your house Nitto once the new one arrives?

"It will be assigned to another family is all."

"That is good then, as long as it does not end up empty and not used."

The rest of the day was spent shopping and getting some warm clothes for all three children. It was fun watching them try on all the bulky clothes and boots. It was shortly after 5 when they again touched down in Sachs Harbour. They pulled the plane inside and they walked Linsey and Jeff to their place then continued down to their small home.

They had a great family day and accomplished all they wanted. Nitto slipped in beside Todd and cuddled close to him. "Todd have you ever thought of having more family?

The question caught him off guard. "At my age Nitto, not all that sure I still have it in me."

Nitto cuddled in close and looked up at him. "You never know Nanuq unless you try," and she blushed. If it is possible I think I would like another child with the man that I love."

Todd smiled at his wife as she lay asleep. He got up and sat in the dark on the couch. He held the card everyone had signed before he had come North. Tears ran down his cheeks as he thought of the way life could have turned if he had not stumbled into the mission that day. Life had its way of taking care of those who cared enough to love the Father above. He was indeed a blessed man.

"The End Of Book One

"Epilogue"

Life has an interesting way of coming around full circle for us. Often we focus on the hardships and fail to look at the reality of the fact we are truly blessed.

I encourage each of you to stop and think for a few moments of just how blessed we truly are. Yes there are some who suffer such as Todd Morris suffered.

In the end life can be like his in many ways and in varying degrees of pain and suffering. We can blame all of those people in our lives of we can look at ourselves and ask what is it I can change to make a difference.

Your attitude, the way you respond to the hard things in life can make such and impact. Take the time to seek deep within and ask what can I do to change.

I can be reached at woodcarver2009@me.com

I welcome your questions and input and will answer all your emails. Thank you for your support and know that you are dearly loved.

"Rolly A. Chabot

Born and raised in Alberta, Canada, after leaving home at an early age I ventured into the far Northern reaches of Canada living in many very remote locations. I finally settled in the Yukon Territory, just above the 60th Parallel. This was a land I began to love, not meant for the fainthearted but made for adventure.

I have written seven books called "Quiet Reflections" of my time there. They are written of the many people who found their way into my life, of the many adventures and of the faithful dog who followed with me through the good and the bad times.

I would be dropped into these regions by a friend by helicopter and would spend as much as three weeks alone in the far reaches of the untouched wilderness. Some of the most wonderful experiences away from all things in life would happen in these places, where creation would speak many things into a man. Understanding the complexity of nature builds something deep into ones spirit. What you understand will determine your survival 200 miles away from the closest man. No cell phone, computer or means of communications.

I invite you to come along with Tannis and I as we meet the people, travel to places where nature speaks volumes of love and peace.

After this seven book series was completed I switched to a Christian/Fiction genre and have completed an additional 13 full length novels. "Smoothwolf 1 and 2 have been added. They are of a young Native American who experienced a hard start in life and found his success in the business world and in love. They have been very successful.

Thank you again and be Blessed
Rolly A. Chabot

www.ingramcontent.com/pod-product-compliance
Lightning Source LLC
Chambersburg PA
CBHW070823180626
46818CB00001B/369